E. Harbour

PRAISE FOR ELMER KELTON

Badger Boy

"Award-winning writer Elmer Kelton—a star in the shrinking Western genre—totes you effortlessly to the post–Civil War Texas frontier, where white settlers were just learning to live with freed slaves, Comanches and each other.... His characters, like Shannon, make mistakes, are far from perfect and take life in stride." —*The New York Post*

"Kelton is a master of both plot and character development, and his Rusty Shannon is a down-to-earth, dusty cowboy whose exploits always thrill Kelton's fans."

—*Publishers Weekly* (starred review)

"In 1995, the Western Writers of America voted San Angelo's Elmer Kelton the best all-time crafter of Western-themed fiction. *Badger Boy* reinforces its author's already glittering reputation.... Kelton himself would disavow any pretension to literary greatness. What he does here, as always, is tell an entertaining story about the West. Longtime fans will be pleased, and newcomers to Kelton's work will realize what they've been missing."

—*The San Jose Mercury News*

"Elmer Kelton's clear, clean prose and compelling plot make *Badger Boy* a terrific read, as one of the most honored Western writers ever vividly potrays the physical hardships and inner struggles of Confederate veteran Rusty Shannon's efforts to rebuild his life on the Red River."

—*The Dallas Morning News*

D0092515

The Buckskin Line

"Having written more than forty novels, Elmer Kelton has surely established himself as one of the grand masters of Western literature. A preeminent storyteller, Kelton has been blessed with the ability to create a cast of fictional characters which bring history to life with such honesty and believability that the reader himself literally becomes part of the story. And so it is with the author's latest offering, *The Buckskin Line*. . . . It is Kelton's understanding of human weaknesses and strengths that make his writings so captivating. From this perspective, the reader is able to understand both sides of a conflict thus gaining a quiet empathy with the challenges each character must face. *The Buckskin Line* is a fascinating new direction for Kelton's work, and one that is certain to have a sequel."

—*The El Paso Scene*

"Carefully researched and realistically presented. This picture of 1860s Texas, with its strong people, tells yet another good story about our state and our ancestors."　　　　—*Austin American-Statesman*

JOE PEPPER

Forge Books by Elmer Kelton

Badger Boy
Bitter Trail
The Buckskin Line
Buffalo Wagons
Cloudy in the West
Hard Trail to Follow
Hot Iron
Jericho's Road
Joe Pepper
Many a River
The Pumpkin Rollers
The Raiders: Sons of Texas
Ranger's Trail
The Rebels: Sons of Texas
Six Bits a Day
The Smiling Country
Sons of Texas
Texas Rifles
Texas Vendetta
The Way of the Coyote

Lone Star Rising
(comprising *The Buckskin Line, Badger Boy,*
and *The Way of the Coyote*)

Brush Country
(comprising *Barbed Wire* and *Llano River*)

Texas Showdown
(comprising *Pecos Crossing* and *Shotgun*)

Texas Sunrise
(comprising *Massacre at Golidad* and *After the Bugles*)

Elmer Kelton

JOE PEPPER

FORGE®

A TOM DOHERTY ASSOCIATES BOOK
NEW YORK

NOTE: If you purchased this book without a cover you should be aware that this book is stolen property. It was reported as "unsold and destroyed" to the publisher, and neither the author nor the publisher has received any payment for this "stripped book."

This is a work of fiction. All the characters and events portrayed in this book are either products of the author's imagination or are used fictitiously.

JOE PEPPER

Copyright © 1975 by Elmer Kelton

All rights reserved.

This book was originally published under Elmer Kelton's pseudonym of Lee McElroy.

A Forge Book
Published by Tom Doherty Associates, LLC
175 Fifth Avenue
New York, NY 10010

www.tor-forge.com

Forge® is a registered trademark of Tom Doherty Associates, LLC.

ISBN 978-0-8125-6157-9

First Forge Edition: May 2002

Printed in the United States of America

0 9 8 7 6 5 4

JOE PEPPER

Chapter 1

Well, preacher, if you've come to pray over me in my last hours, I'm afraid it's too late. I've seen a few of them last-minute conversions, and I never put much stock in them. I doubt as the Lord does, either. But I'm grateful for your company anyway. Looks like they're going to hammer on that scaffold out there all night, so I won't be getting no sleep. Far as I'm concerned they could put it off a day or two and not work so hard.

Don't be bashful. If you want to hear my story, all you got to do is ask for it. It can't be used against me now. I've seen what they said was my story lots of times, written up in the newspapers and penny-dreadfuls. Lies, most of them. Some reporter listens to a few wild rumors, gets him a pencil, some paper and a jug, and he writes the *whole true story* of Joe Pepper, big bad gunfighter of the wild West. Damn liars, most of them newspaper people. Tell one of them the time of day and he'll set his watch wrong.

I think I know what you're after . . . you'd like to

have the story straight so you can tell it to your congregation. Maybe it'll scare some of them twisty boys and turn them aside from the paths of iniquity. It might at that, though I can't say I've wasted much time regretting the things I've done. My main regret has been over some men I didn't shoot when I had the chance.

Don't expect me to give you the dates, and maybe I'll disremember a name or two. I figure a man's head can just hold so much information, and he'd better not fill it up with a lot of unnecessaries.

I've always liked to tell people I was born in Texas, but since you're a preacher I won't lie to you. I always wished *I was* born in Texas. The truth is that I was born just across the line in Louisiana. My daddy and mama, they could look across the river and *see* Texas; they was of that old-time Texian breed, and it was just an accident of war that I wasn't born where I was supposed to be. You've heard of the great Runaway Scrape? That was after Santa Anna and them Mexicans wiped out the Alamo and massacred all of them soldiers at Goliad. The settlers, they lit out in a wild run for the Sabine River to get across into the United States before Santa Anna could overtake them.

Now, my daddy was in Sam Houston's army for a while, leaving my mama with some neighbors on the land he had claimed in Austin's colony. But when the Scrape started, he got to fretting about her, knowing she was nigh to term. Didn't look then like Sam Houston intended to fight anyway; he just kept backing off, letting Santa Anna come on and on. So my daddy deserted and rushed my mama across into Louisiana where she would be safe. While he was there, Sam Houston and his bunch whipped the britches off of Santa Anna at San Jacinto. Daddy missed out on that. He also missed out on the league and *labor* of land that the Republic of Texas granted to all the San Jacinto soldiers. If he'd of been in on that, we'd of been a lot more prosperous than we ever was.

The rest of his life he always told people he had been a soldier under Sam Houston. He didn't tell them about the deserting, and the Runaway Scrape.

When the war was over my folks went back to the farm, and of course I was with them by then. You'll hear people who don't know no better bragging about what a wonderful grand thing it was, the Republic of Texas. Either they don't know or they're so old and senile that they've forgot. It was a cruel, hard time. There wasn't no money to be had, hardly, and most people had to grub deep just to hold body and soul together. Seems to me like the first thing I can remember is following my mama and daddy down the rows of a cottonfield. Time I was old enough to take hold of a hoehandle, they had one ready for me. Only time I ever laid it down in the daylight was to take hold of something heavier. I remember watching my folks grow old before their time, trying their best not to lose that little old place.

I was grown and hiring out for plowman's wages when the War between the States come on. I was a good marksman like everybody else in that country then; most of the meat we ever had on the table was wild game that I went out and shot. There was people that used to run hogs loose along the rivers and creeks, living off of the acorns and such. Every once in a while I would shoot me one of those and tell the folks it was a wild one. They wouldn't of eaten it no other way. Religious folks they was; they'd of taken a liking to you, preacher. But I always felt like the Lord helped them that helped theirselves, and I helped myself any time it come handy.

Well, like I say, the war started. Right off, I volunteered. My old daddy, he joined up too. It had always gnawed at him, I reckon, that he wasn't there when Sam Houston won that other war. He wanted to be in on this one. So he left Mama and the kids to take care of the place, and him and me went off to war. He never did get there, though. We hadn't been gone from home three weeks till he was taken down with the fever and

died without ever seeing a Yankee. We gave him a
Christian burial three hundred miles from home. I always wanted to go back someday and put up a stone, but
I never could find the place, not within five miles. Probably fenced into somebody's cow pasture now.

The war wasn't nothing I like to talk about. My part in
it wasn't much different from most any other soldier's. I
taken three bullet wounds, one time and another. I killed
a few men that had never done nothing against me except shoot at me. Maybe that sounds funny to you, but
it's true. There wasn't nothing personal in it; they was
shooting at *everybody* that wore a uniform the color of
mine. They didn't know me from Robert E. Lee. It was
our job to kill more of them than they killed of us.

Everybody seemed to feel like it was all right for me
to shoot strangers in the war, but in later years they got
awful self-righteous. Some wanted to hang me when I'd
shot a man that *did* have a personal fight with me, men
that wanted to kill Joe Pepper, only Joe Pepper beat
them to it. Folks would say I'd forgotten the war was
over. Well, it never *was* over for me. Seems like I've
been in one war or another most of my life. I never could
get it straight, them changing the rules on me all the
time.

I was way over in Pennsylvania when the war was
over and they told us to go home. I had taken a good sorrel horse off of a dead Yankee, but that chicken-brained
captain of ours led us into an ambush that a blind mule
could've seen, and the horse got shot out from under me.
The best officers we had got killed off in the first years
of the war, seemed like, and mostly what we had left in
the last part was the scrubs and the cutbacks. The night
after they told us to go home, I slipped along the picket
line and taken a good big gray horse of the captain's. I
figured he owed me that for getting my sorrel shot. I
knowed he wouldn't take the same view on it, though, so
I was thirty miles toward Texas by daylight.

That horse was the making of my first fortune, in a manner of speaking. Big stout horse he was, about fifteen hands high, Tennessee stock. Once I had schooled him, I could rope a full-grown range bull on him and he'd bust that bull over backwards. But that was later on, of course. That was when I was still known as Joe Peeler. The Joe Pepper name came later.

When I got back to the old homeplace I found out Mama had died, and the kids was taking care of the farm themselves. Couple of the boys was grown and plenty able. They didn't have no need of me, and one thing they *didn't* need was an extra mouth to feed. So I taken off and headed south with an old army friend of mine, Arlee Thompson. He had come from below San Antonio in the Nueces Strip country. That was a rough territory them days, Mexican outlaws coming across the line to see what they could take and run with, American outlaws settling there so if they was pressed they could always run for Mexico. The honest people—what there was of them—had a hard time. Even the honest ones fought amongst theirselves a right smart, *Americanos* against Mexicans and *vice versa*. You'd of thought they had trouble enough without that, but they didn't seem to think so.

The ranches had let a lot of their cattle go unbranded through the war because there just wasn't enough men to do the job. There was grown cattle there—bulls three and four years old that had never felt knife or iron— cows with their second or third calf at side, their ears and hides as slick as the calves' were. Cattle wasn't worth much in them first times after the war, hardly worth anybody fighting over. People fought anyway, of course. Men'll fight when they can't even *eat*. Me and Arlee, we figured there'd be money in cattle again. We set out to claim as many as we could. *Mavericking* is what we called it them days, after a man named Maverick who said all the branded cattle belonged to the man who registered the brand, and all the unbranded cattle belonged to *him*.

Now, there was some people who didn't take kindly to what we done. You ever hear of Jesse Ordway? He was a power in that lower country. He didn't go to war himself, so he was sitting down there putting things together while most of the men was off fighting Yankees. He gobbled up a lot of that country, taking it away from the Mexicans, buying out war widows for a sack of cornmeal and such like. He didn't object to people branding mavericks as long as they was working for him and burning *his* brand on them, but it sure did put the gravel under his skin to see other people doing it. He thought he had him a nice private little hunting preserve. The rest of us was poachers.

But damn good poachers we was. Inside of a year me and Arlee had us a pretty good-sized herd of cattle apiece. We didn't own an acre of ground, either one of us, but half the people down there didn't. Jesse Ordway didn't actually own a fraction of what he claimed. Most of it he just squatted on and used because he was bigger and stronger than anybody else and had the gall to hold it.

I didn't tell you yet about Arlee's sister. Millie was her name. Arlee wasn't much to look at, tall and thin and bent over a little, and had a short scar over one cheek where a Yankee bullet kind of winked at him as it went by. But Millie, she must've took after her mother's side of the family. I've got a picture of her here in the back of my watch. See, wasn't she the prettiest thing ever you laid your eyes on? Picture's faded a little, but take my word for it. She wasn't much bigger than a minute, and had light-colored hair that reminded me a little of corn silk. And eyes? The bluest eyes that ever melted a miser's heart.

She was living with her old daddy on the place he had claimed as his share from the revolution. It was a

league and a *labor* just like they'd of given *my* daddy if
he had stayed with Sam Houston. But the old man
Thompson had had his share of hard luck and had lost
most of his country one way and another. He was down
to just a little hard-scrabble outfit about big enough to
chunk rocks at a dog on. Time me and Arlee got there,
he was most blind, and it was up to Millie and a Mexican
hand named Felipe Rios to take care of the work. Jesse
Ordway had branded up a lot of the old man's calves for
himself, and there wasn't much the old man or that Mexican boy could do about it. The old man prayed a good
deal, asking the Lord to forgive Ordway because he
knowed not what he done.

You'll have to pardon me, preacher, but that's one
thing I never could accept about these religious people,
always asking forgiveness for their enemies. Ordway
knew what he was doing, and he didn't need forgiveness; what he needed was a damn good killing.

First time I seen Millie I couldn't believe she was Arlee's sister. But there was a resemblance; they both had
the same big blue innocent eyes. You could've told either one of them that the sun would come up out of the
west tomorrow and they'd believe you. I told Millie a
good many lies at first, till my conscience got to hurting.
People will tell you I never had a conscience, but they
don't know me. It always plagued me when I done
something I thought was wrong. So most of my life I've
tried not to do them things. Other people might've
thought I done wrong, but I don't have to listen to *their*
conscience, just *mine*.

The old man died a little while after I got there. I
reckon he had been ready to go before but had waited till
Arlee was at home to take care of Millie. Old folks are
like that sometimes, you know; they just keep the door
locked against death till they're ready to go, then they
seem to walk out and meet it of their own free will. I've
seen some that greeted it like a friend.

The day came when we got news that the railroad had built west into Kansas, and people in South Texas began to round up a lot of them cattle and drive them north to turn into Yankee dollars. Me and Arlee had us close to two hundred steers apiece over and above the maverick heifers we had put our brands on. The heifers had to stay—they was seed stock for the future. But them steers was excess, a liquid asset like the bankers always say. During our mavericking time we would split them fifty-fifty. We worked together, me and Arlee. We would put his brand on one and mine on the next. Felipe Rios helped us, but he didn't get no cattle. He was working for wages, when we had any money to pay him. Anyway, he was a Mexican. They let Mexicans maverick cattle for other people, but they was stealing if they mavericked for theirselves. They would get their necks lengthened. Sounds rough, but that's the way it was, them days.

Four hundred steers wasn't enough to make up a good trail herd, so we throwed in with some more smaller operators and put together something like thirteen hundred head of cattle.

Jesse Ordway tried to crowd us. He brought in a couple of Rangers and claimed we had stolen a lot of the cattle—me and Arlee and some of the others. He bluffed and blustered, and I reckon he thought he had them Rangers in his pocket, but he didn't. They listened to him real polite, then started asking him to show the proof. That was one thing he couldn't do. The Rangers cussed him out for wasting their time and rode off and left him.

Then he tried to bluff us. He brought a gunfighter he had used to run some of the Mexicans off of their country, a *pistolero* name of Threadgill. He was before your time; you probably never heard of him. He was just a cheap four-flusher anyway. He got by on bluff, not on guts. The only thing game about him was his smell.

Ordway brought Threadgill and some others up to stop us the morning we threw our herd onto the trail. Threadgill was the man out front. The way they had it made up, he was supposed to kill one or two of us and the rest would turn tail and run.

I used to carry my pistol stuck into my belt them days. I never did fancy a holster much. I watched Threadgill's face. Just before he reached for his gun, I could see it coming in his eyes. I didn't try to draw my gun; that would've taken too long. I just left it in the belt and twisted the muzzle up at Threadgill and pulled the trigger. Bullet caught him at about the second button on his shirt. One of them other toughs tried to draw his gun, but a shot come from behind me, and he was already falling before I could get my pistol pointed in his direction.

It was over in about the time it takes a chewing man to spit. There was that big Texas gunfighter Threadgill laying on the ground at Ordway's feet, dead enough to skin. The other one was laying there coughing, going the same way only taking a little longer. I looked around and seen smoke curling up from Felipe Rios's pistol. He had one of them old-fashioned cap-and-ball relics that must of weighed forty pounds.

It would've shamed that hired tough considerable to have knowed he was killed by a Mexican.

I kept my pistol pointed at Ordway's left eye, where he couldn't hardly overlook it. I hoped he would do something foolish, so we could adjourn court right then and there. But he decided not to press the case. He taken the rest of his men and went home, looking like a scalded dog.

The story got noised around, and nobody else in that part of the country gave us any argument. If anything, them old boys came out to help us push our cattle along. A lot of them was glad to see anybody get the best of Jesse Ordway.

I could of shot him right then and there, and later

on I wished I had. It would've saved me and lots of people a right smart of trouble. It taught me a lesson that I didn't forget as the years went by: when in doubt, *kill* the son of a bitch.

We had a pretty easy drive, as cattle drives went; there wasn't none of them real easy. We caught the Red River in flood and lost one of the cowboys there. The average cowboy couldn't swim a lick.

We could've easy had some Indian trouble up in the Nations, but as it turned out we didn't. We run onto a bunch of Indians that thought we ought to give them some of the beeves just for trailing cattle over their land. Arrogant bunch, they was. The only reason they had that land in the first place was that the government gave it to them; they didn't have any business charging taxpaying citizens for traveling across it. Couple of the boys gave them a steer apiece, but they didn't get any of mine.

Nearest we ever come to a real fight was amongst ourselves. There was a fat boy with us who owned something like four hundred head—more than any of the rest of us. Name was Lathrop Nettleton, and he figured that as the biggest owner he ought to ramrod the outfit. None of us paid him much mind. We each of us went about and did what we could see needed to be done, and we mostly just ignored him. He got to mouthing at me one time, and I had to knock him down. I invited him to pull his gun if he was a mind to, but he wasn't. Time we got to Kansas we was all mighty sick of him. I'm proud to say he was just as sick of me.

We pulled into Abilene and got the cattle sold and split up the money according to the cattle count. You ever see one of them trail's end celebrations, preacher? No? Well, that's probably a good thing. I'm here to tell you it's no place for a man of the Gospel. There was other cow outfits in there besides ours, so the whole place was overrun with Texas cowboys trying to wash three months of dust out of their throats with the most damnable whiskey you've ever drunk—begging your pardon again, preacher. And then there was the girls over there on the tracks. I didn't go for none of that, you understand; by that time I had made up my mind I was going to marry Millie Thompson even if I had to carry her off like some Mexican bandit. Her brother Arlee was with me, and I sure didn't want him telling her no tales out of school. So I stayed with the whiskey and played a little cards.

There was a small saloon over next to the railroad that seemed kind of comfortable. It was run by an old-time Union soldier who had lost an arm in the war. I kind of taken a liking to him; I reckon he was the first damnyankee I had ever seen that was cut up enough to suit me. There was one of them Eastern gamblers, too, the kind that always wore a swallowtail coat and a silk hat. I figured he had to be crooked; I never did trust a man that had slick hands and wore a coat in the summertime.

I ought to tell you that I wasn't just the average run-of-the-mill cowboy when it came to cards. In the army I'd spent some time amongst a bunch of Mississippi River boys who could make a deck of cards do just about anything but sing "Dixie." I had learned a right smart from them, at no small expense to myself. Still, I didn't think I wanted to try that Eastern gambler on for size. I never could understand them cowboys that knew they was outclassed but still would go up against one of them sharps. Playing for matches on a saddle-blanket is a lot different from playing for blood on one of them slick tables.

Some of the boys from our drive wanted to play him. Normally I'd of tried to talk them out of it, but Lathrop Nettleton was amongst them, and I figured it would do me good to see him nailed to the wall. So I just sat there and watched them play. I knowed sooner or later that gambler was going to suck them boys under and drown them like a coon drowns a hunting dog.

He was smooth about it. He taken his time before he set the hook. He'd win a hand and then let one of the other boys win one. Seemed like for a while he was losing more chips than he was taking in, so pretty soon some extra hands from other outfits sat in on the game. Gradually he got to winning. Along about midnight he was taking all the chips. Some of the boys had sense enough to draw out before they lost it all, but Lathrop Nettleton just hung and rattled to the bitter end. Before that gambler got through with him Nettleton had lost everything those four hundred steers had brought him. He was lucky to have a saddlehorse to ride home on. The gambler gave him back twenty dollars' worth of chips. "For seed," he says. "I want to see you back here again next year."

I might've felt sorry for Nettleton then if he hadn't started to beg. That was one thing I never could stand to see a man do. The one-armed barkeep finally had to put him out of there; told him if he couldn't afford to lose, he couldn't afford to play.

I didn't interfere. I could of told Nettleton if I'd wanted to that I had been watching the gambler palm cards all night.

The boys was pretty well whipped down. The gambler set them all up to a drink at the bar before they went back to their wagons. Nettleton was already gone. I just sat there at the table by myself, glad Arlee hadn't been in the game. When the boys finished their drink and started for the door they asked me if I was coming with them, I told them no, I wasn't quite ready for the bedroll yet.

That gambler knowed I had money on me. When there was just him and me and the barkeep left in the place, he says to me, "The night's still in her youth. Like to play a few hands, just me and you?"

I slipped that pistol out of my belt and pointed it up in the general direction of his Adam's apple. It got to working up and down. "So that's it," he says. "You're going to rob me."

I says to him, "No, the robbery has already taken place. If I'd of told them boys they'd of tore you to pieces and fed you to the dogs. I thought the best thing was to stay here till they was gone and give you a chance to square things up without throwing your life into forfeit."

He blustered and bluffed about not being a cheater, but I had him cold, and he knowed it. He finally caved in. I told him the only fair thing was for him to give back all the money he had won from the boys. I said it might help their feelings if he throwed in a little extra for interest. He turned kind of clabber-colored, but he shoved all the chips across the table. I got the barkeep to cash them.

I told that gambler if I was him I wouldn't wait around for daylight. "Getting their money back won't be enough for the boys," I says. "They're liable to come hunting for you. Smart thing would be to get you a horse and leave now. You could be a long ways up the track before sunup, and I'd be a few days coming back if I was you."

That one-armed saloonkeeper seen it pretty much the way I did and seconded all my advice. He said they was good people, them Texas cowboys, when they was on your side. But they was woolly boogers when they was against you. That gambler walked out of there with nothing much besides his silk hat and that swallowtail coat and whatever cards was still up his sleeve. I had all his money.

You couldn't say I lied to him, exactly. I didn't exactly tell him I *was* going to give the boys their money back. I just sort of let him believe that was the way it was going to be. But the way I seen it, it wouldn't be fair to give the money back to the rest of the boys if I didn't give it to Nettleton too. I didn't want to be dishonest about the thing, so I just kept all the money for myself.

I never told Arlee Thompson the whole truth. I told him I'd had me a set-to with the gambler after the rest of the boys got through, and that I had better luck than they did. I didn't let on to Arlee how much money I really had till we got back to South Texas. I had all my share of the cattle money, minus the little bit I had spent on whiskey and new clothes, and I had all the money off of that poker table. It was a pretty good road stake for them days.

I was a little afraid some of the boys would go back over there the next day and find out from that Yankee barkeep what had happened. Things could of got a little unpleasant. But none of them seemed like they wanted to ever see the place again. They didn't have the money to be going back there anyway, most of them. They'd had their plow cleaned.

We passed Jesse Ordway's trail herd heading north as we went south, going home. We had got out on the trail a long ways ahead of him and sold our cattle early in the season when the price was at about its peak. First ones there generally lapped the cream, and the late ones taken the skim milk. I know Ordway wasn't none too pleased to see us. Them days it was custom to invite passing strangers to stop for a meal or two—even the night—at your wagon. But Ordway didn't give us any invite. I didn't let it worry me. I was already way ahead of him because some of the mavericks I had branded had been his once upon a time; he was so busy branding other people's that he hadn't got around to all of his own. It was the quick that won the marbles them days, and the slow just wasn't in it at all.

Naturally we got home several weeks ahead of Ordway, and I didn't let no grass grow under my feet. I had done a lot of thinking about Millie Thompson. I'd lay awake at night and imagine I could hear her talking to me, laughing with me. She had a voice that kind of lifted sometimes and broke and sounded like a hundred little silver bells tinkling. It doesn't take much of that to set a young man to making all kinds of dreams and plans. I wanted to build her a home and live in it with her for a thousand years.

I had kept that money a secret. When we got back to South Texas I went to listening and looking, and pretty soon through Felipe Rios I found out there was three-four Mexican families wanting to sell out. Felipe was telling them they ought to stay and fight, but he was just a bachelor, and they was family men. Jesse Ordway had been pushing on them pretty hard, running off their cattle, burning their hay, scaring their womenfolk. Not himself, understand, but people he hired for that kind of thing. They knew when he got back off of his trail drive that they was fixing to catch hell. They couldn't look to the law for help. Them lawmen wouldn't take two steps out of their way to help a Mexican.

Without acting too interested I managed to find out what Ordway had been offering them. When I figured out the places I wanted and could afford, I went and bought them. Them Mexicans thought I was one *crazy gringo*, but they was tickled to take my money and run. One of them told me Jesse Ordway would be shoveling dirt in my face before the first cold norther of the winter. But I reckon he figured it was better mine than his, because he was sure glad to take what I offered him.

I oughtn't to've been, but I was some surprised to find out that Millie Thompson wanted to marry me as much as I wanted to marry her. I had thought I might have to argue with her. You wouldn't think so to see me like I am now, an old man, but there was some folks—women anyway—who used to say I was handsome them days. I never was one to argue much with a woman.

We had us a church wedding with all the trimmings.

Surprise you, preacher? Bet from all the things you heard about me, you thought I was never in church in my life. But I was, once or twice before that and at least once since that I can remember. There was a time long years ago when I climbed up into a church loft to get away from a bunch of angry old boys that was after me, but there wasn't no praying done that time, not that I recall.

We took us a short wedding trip to San Antonio . . . stayed in the best suite of rooms we could get in the Menger Hotel, just down the hall from where Captain Richard King himself was holding forth. The *King Ranch* King, you know. Looking at him, I even taken a notion that if I worked extra hard and played my cards right, I might get to be as big a man in the cattle business someday as he was.

You a married man? Then I suppose you know how sweet things was for me and Millie for a while. That picture I showed you in the back of my watch . . . she had that made in San Antonio. You can see the sparkle in her eyes if you look close. Oh, that was a happy time.

I never completely put Jesse Ordway out of my mind, though. I kind of kept track of where I thought he would be, one day to the next. I had us a crew of carpenters camping out and building us a house before Ordway ever got home. Naturally he taken the Lord's name in vain when he found out what I had done. The places I picked was all on the river. The Mexicans had been doing a little irrigation, and there was a lot more good land that a man could have put into farms if he had the inclination and the strong back to do it. Ordway had figured on taking that land dirt cheap and growing a lot of feed on it so he could run even more cows than he already had. And I had come along and set myself square down in the middle of his road.

Couple days after he got home he came over to the place where I had the carpenters working. It was like

he didn't even see that house, like all he could see was
me, and he sure didn't appreciate the view. He told me
I had as much as stolen the land from him, and I told
him I had bought it free and clear from the previous
rightful owners, and now I had all the papers to show
that I was the present rightful owner, and he could go
soak his head in a muddy tank.

He says to me, "You know what I mean. You'll have
no luck here. You'd do a lot better to move far away
and start over." He offered to buy the land from me at
seventy-five cents on the dollar. The other twenty-five
percent I could mark down on the books as a fee for
education.

By this time he had hired him another gunhand, a
beady-eyed *pistolero* named Sorrells. You probably
never heard of him. He had a right smart of a local
reputation, but that was a long time ago. This Sorrells
sat on his horse alongside Ordway. Dun horse it was,
best I can recollect; I remember thinking to myself that
if anybody was to shoot Sorrells—which was more
than likely—maybe I could buy that horse off of the
sheriff. Sorrells didn't say nothing, just sat there and
tried to look mean. I taken him to be of about the same
caliber as Threadgill, the other one Ordway had sicced
onto me, and I had salted him away without no sweat
on my part.

I told Ordway I'd buy *him* out at fifty cents on the
dollar, which would've been a good deal on his part
because he didn't own half of what he claimed. I'd of
had to steal the money someplace if he had taken me
up, but I was satisfied I could do it. Ordway just stared
at me, hard. Sorrells kept looking from me to Ordway
and back to me again, waiting for Ordway to tell him
to go ahead and kill me. He was awful anxious to earn
his wages; I reckon he liked to see that a man got his
money's worth. But Ordway had a pretty good memory, and maybe he thought I'd of shot him as well as

Sorrells if he'd of given me the excuse. He was right;
I sure as hell would.

Felipe Rios was there too, a few steps off to one side
of me.

Ordway caved. He backed his horse up a little and
told me I'd better chew on it and be awful careful of
my luck. I could tell when they rode away that Sorrells
was disappointed. Some people just naturally enjoy
their work more than others do.

Me and Millie had been sleeping in one of the old
Mexican houses while we waited for our new one to
be finished. Fresh married like we was, it didn't make
a particle of difference where we slept. The days was
way too long anyhow, seemed like, and the nights too
short.

Well, that night turned out to be long enough. The
Mexican house was maybe two hundred yards from
where the new one was going up. Sometime about midnight I heard shooting. I jumped out of bed and grabbed
my britches. The shooting stopped before I could get
my pants and boots on and run outside. I could see the
new house was afire. I could see people running around
down there, and I could hear horses. I couldn't shoot
because I was apt to hit the carpenters or Felipe; he
was camped down there with them. I heard the horses
loping away in the dark and men hollering in Mexican.
But they wasn't Mexicans, I could tell. A man don't
need much of an ear to tell when it's some *gringo*
trying to *talk* Mexican.

There wasn't nothing we could do to save the house.
It was plumb gone. So was one of the carpenters; they
had put so much lead in him that it taken two extra
pallbearers to carry him. Felipe wanted to chase after
them, but Millie was scared for me to leave her alone.

Next day I called out the law. They said it was Mexican bandits. I knowed they knowed better, and I
cussed them for a bunch of chicken-livered cowards.

But they was local, and they was afraid of Jesse Ordway.

I thought once that I was going to get even. Ordway was married; had him a thin, shivery little woman he had found over in San Antonio teaching in a church school. Reminded me of a scared rabbit locked up in a cage. She was as afraid of Jesse Ordway as she would've been of a rattlesnake. They had a boy about seven or eight years old, and it seemed to me like he took after his mama more than his daddy. Didn't seem like there was any fight in her or in the boy either. His daddy would say something, and that boy would cringe like a pup that's had the whip put to him.

Anyhow, Ordway was on a kind of house-building spree of his own. His was going to be a lot bigger than mine would've been. For a while I had a notion of going over there and burning it down some night, but that wouldn't of paid me back anything. And after what he had done to me I knowed he would have it guarded like a vault full of gold bars. There was an easier way of getting him.

I found out he was having the lumber hauled down from San Antonio. Me and Felipe went out on the road one day and got the drop on them freighters and persuaded them to haul one whole shipment over to my place. I figured Ordway owed me that, and I also figured if he came to get it back it might give me a good excuse to kill him.

He didn't even try. He didn't have to, because that lumber never done me no good. I couldn't hire a carpenter anywhere in the country to start building that house back. The word had gotten around. I'd of built it myself, but a saw and a hammer just never did fit my hands. Millie had to keep living in that old Mexican house. She never once complained about it. That nice frame house had been my idea in the first place, not hers.

Things was quiet till into the fall of the year. I had

about decided Ordway had given up on me till one day
he rode up with three or four hands, and the gunfighter
Sorrells at his side. He taken a look at the pile of his
lumber laying out there, but he didn't say anything
about it. He taken a lot longer look at the rifle I had
in my hands, pointed about six inches below his collar-
button. He told me that sure wasn't any polite way to
treat company, and I told him I never treated *company*
that way. He offered to buy me out for the money I
had invested in my place. That was a twenty-five percent better offer than his first one, but I told him that
wouldn't allow me any pay for the time and labor I
had already put in.

He didn't seem inclined to raise the ante. He just
told me what he had said the last time, that I'd better
be careful of my luck.

I knowed he would have a hell of a time burning
down the Mexican house because it was of adobe, and
the roof had a covering of dried mud on it. He might
melt it down, if he could make that much water, but
he would never burn it down.

They hit us that same night. I can't say it was by
surprise, because we sort of expected them. The surprise was that there was so many of them. I found out
later that he didn't use his regular hands because he
didn't want any of them talking when it was over. He
went down to the border and hired him a bunch of
renegades from the other side that he knowed wouldn't
come back and incriminate him. So the ones that hit
us that night was him and Sorrells and them renegades.

All I had was myself and Felipe and a couple of
hands that I had hired to work cattle, not fight. They
didn't do much fighting; they turned and ran. Felipe
got shot in the leg in the first charge; he was sleeping
out under an open arbor and couldn't get to the house
in time. They swarmed over him and clubbed him and
left him for dead. So then it was just me, with Millie
loading my guns.

They tried first to set the place afire, but there wasn't much that would burn. Every time one of them would come charging up with a torch I would either hit him or come so close that he would drop the thing and run. They gave it up directly and set in to trying to cut the house to pieces. They shot out all the windows in the first few minutes—they was of wood, not glass—but them thick adobe walls stopped most of the bullets. Now and then one would bust through, but most of them either glanced off or stuck in the mud blocks.

There wasn't but one door to the place, and we had it barred. The only way they could come in was through that door or one of the front windows. They might've made it if they had had the nerve to gang up and all rush us at one time. But I reckon they knowed a bunch of them would die in the trying. They sat out there and potshotted at the windows, and I knowed we had them beat.

Then it happened. One of them slugs came right through the wall. The wall was of a double thickness of mud blocks, but I reckon there was a few places where the mud mortar on two blocks was on the same level. It was soft enough that the bullet came through.

Millie screamed. God, preacher, you never heard such a scream in your life. It hit her just under the heart. I had just time to catch her before she fell. All I could do was lay her out on the dirt floor and straighten her legs. She clutched at my shirt and cried out one more time; it must've hurt her something terrible. Then she was gone.

My Millie—my pretty Millie—was dead.

The shooting had stopped. They had all heard the scream. I heard a voice I knowed was Ordway's, telling them to rush the house. They just stayed put. Way I heard it later, that scream froze their blood, most of them, and the few others didn't want to try to swarm the house by theirselves. Ordway was out there in the dark, cussing a blue streak at them in Spanish and English both, because some was white and some was Mexican. Finally a couple of them made a run for the door. I dropped one of them six feet from the house; the other turned and ran. It was too dark to be sure, but I thought it was probably Sorrells.

After that I heard them pulling out. Ordway was telling them they wouldn't be paid a cent if they didn't go through with their bargain, but they rode off and left him. Directly everything out there got quiet. I sat myself down on the floor and taken Millie's hand and just held it for the longest time. I'm not ashamed to tell you, preacher, I cried like a baby. And when I was done crying, I sat there and talked to her like if she could of heard me, telling her what all plans I had had, and how much I loved her.

A long time after, I heard a noise and thought maybe they had come back. I got my rifle and eased the door open and waited, hoping they would try another rush so I could see just how many of them I could kill.

It was Felipe Rios crawling along, pulling himself a few inches at a time.

I helped him inside, and he saw Millie, and he crossed himself the way all them Catholics do, and he said something that sounded a little like Spanish but wasn't. I got him wrapped up the best I could in the dark; it was too risky to light a lamp. Then we waited for morning to come. It was one of the longest nights I ever spent in my life.

The two hands who had run away from us had done one decent thing, at least; they went to town and fetched the law. They didn't figure to find me alive, or they wouldn't of ever come back. I cussed them up one side and down the other and told them if I ever seen either one of them again I'd kill him like a dog. At the time, I meant it.

Word got to Arlee Thompson somehow, and he came over in a hard lope. He taken it pretty hard about Millie.

The law was no more help to me that time than they had been before. They declared the whole thing was the work of Mexican bandits who had surely gotten back across the river by now. I told them it was Ordway, that I'd heard his voice, but they told me I was mistaken. The last thing they wanted to do was to tangle up with Jesse Ordway. He could of stolen the county courthouse piece by piece and they'd of fetched him a wagon.

It taken me a while to figure out what to do about Ordway. What I really wanted was to go over there and just shoot him down. But I would never of been allowed to live that long.

We buried Millie on her old family homeplace. Arlee thought that was kind of strange, but I told him I wouldn't be keeping my land, and I wanted her to rest in her own ground where maybe there would be kin around through the times to come.

I sent word to Ordway that if he still wanted to buy me out, I'd sell to him on the terms of his last offer. I wanted cold hard cash because I figured on leaving the country. I didn't want no check, draft, or bank order. He sent me word what day to meet him in town at the bank with the deeds ready to sign over.

Felipe Rios was still weak. He had to have a crutch to walk, and he had to be helped onto a horse. But in the saddle he could handle himself pretty good. After all the help he had been, I hated to just leave him flat. I arranged with Arlee to give him a job. The morning I left for town I told Felipe to go to Arlee's. He wanted to go to town with me, but I told him he didn't have no business there, and he'd better do what I said. When I headed down the town road, I looked back once and seen him heading out in the direction of Arlee's.

I seen half a dozen O Bar horses tied at racks along the street. In front of the bank was a rig with Ordway's brand painted on it. Ordway's little boy sat up there all by himself. I figured he had been told to stay out of

the bank, and he was way too young to wait in one
of the saloons or Mexican *cantinas*. I rode straight up
to the rack nearest to the bank door. I stopped and
looked at the boy. He seemed to be a little afraid of
me, because he kind of shrunk up on the seat of that
rig. I asks him, "You a pretty good cowhand, son?"

He shook his head without saying anything, and I
told him it was a thing a man could learn if he had to.
I unfastened my saddlebags.

In the bank, Jesse Ordway was waiting for me. He
had Sorrells there with him, maybe figuring I might
come in shooting. But I didn't, and I could see in Sorrells's eyes that he was laughing at me. They had
beaten me, and he was enjoying it. Maybe Ordway was
enjoying it too, in his way, but he was more interested
in business. With him it wasn't the principle of the
thing; it was the money. He didn't try to shake hands
with me; I wouldn't of done it noway. He says to me,
"We have everything ready for you to sign. And I have
the money all counted out for you. Sorry about your
wife."

That was the order he ranked everything in. The
money first.

I looked around the bank. Over to one side I seen
Ordway's wife sitting near the bank president's desk.
She was the same as every time I had ever seen her,
scared. I had wondered a time or two how come she
ever married such a man in the first place, because it
was plain there wasn't no love lost for either one of
them. I figured maybe she was too scared of him to
say *no*. I wondered what she was in the bank for, and
then I remembered that as the wife she was probably
expected to sign papers.

Seeing her there kind of brought things back to me
in a rush. Ordway's wife was alive, but mine was dead.
And he had been responsible for killing her.

I tipped my hat to Mrs. Ordway and bowed a little,
the way we was all taught to do, them days. I says,
"Sorry my wife's not here to visit with you." I suppose
I meant a little malice, because she must of known

what her husband had done. She looked down and mumbled something I couldn't hear.

Ordway says, "Something's got to be done to stop those Mexican bandits."

I knowed he was a liar, and he knowed I knowed it. I seen a hard smile come across Sorrells's face.

Ordway says, "Too bad you didn't sell out earlier. All that misfortune would not have befallen you."

You know what hate tastes like? It's got a flavor all its own, not like salt, not like pepper, not like gall. It's not like anything else I know. I tasted it then like I've never tasted it another time in my life.

I laid out what papers I had, and he laid out some legal agreements he had had a lawyer draw up. I never could figure out lawyer talk; I always suspected it was just a code they make up to rob the rest of us with. It didn't matter; the money stacked on that table did all the talking I needed to finish the deal. Ordway says, "It's all counted out."

I told him I'd count it myself, just to be sure. They had it in big denominations, twenty- and fifty-dollar bills. I doubted that this little cowtown bank had had all those bills on hand; they had probably had to send to San Antonio after them. It came out to about the same amount of money I had had when I first got home from that trail drive to Abilene, plus fifteen dollars a head for about two hundred cows I had mavericked or run a new brand on. There was probably more cattle than that, but the deal didn't call for a physical count, just range delivery.

I says, "This don't take into account the improvements." There hadn't been many, really. I had just fixed up some old pens and trap fences that was there to begin with but was run down some.

Ordway didn't seem too inclined to argue. He says, "All right, I'll add a thousand dollars."

It was too easy. I'd always found that when a man just up and gives you something, you'd better watch him because he's probably figuring to give you something *else* you didn't bargain on. I looked into Ordway's eyes, and I knew. It didn't matter what he paid me; he didn't intend to let me get out of this country alive. Once we finished this deal, I was as good as dead, and he would get most of his money back ... maybe all of it.

I decided I had just as well take all I could get. I didn't really have any extra horses, but I didn't see where a little lie right there could hurt anything. I told him I had twenty head that hadn't been counted into the deal. He could have them for fifty dollars apiece or I would drive them to San Antonio and sell them. He motioned to the banker, and they counted me out another thousand dollars.

I put all the money into the saddlebags and then buckled the flaps down tight. I seen Ordway looking at them bags the way a hungry cat looks at a bird. I started to take them, and Ordway laid his hands across one of them. "The papers first," he says. "You got to sign the papers."

The deeds was all spread out there on the table. I wrote my name everywhere the banker told me, then blew on the ink to make it dry.

Ordway taken his hand off of the bag then. He had a look like a cat which had just got the bird in his mouth.

I says, "Jesse Ordway, you're a greedy man. Just what makes you want all this land so bad?"

He looked at his wife, then looked out the door toward where his son was still sitting in the rig. He says, "I got a family. I'm trying to build something worthwhile that I can leave to my son."

You ever notice that's what all them old land-hogs used to say? They was never building anything for theirselves, if you heard them tell it. They was always doing it for somebody else. The milk of human kindness was bubbling up and overflowing out of their hearts. Charity to the core. But they'd kill you for that charity if you got in their way.

I pushed my chair back away from the table and stood up. I says, "Ordway, I hope you're ready."

"Ready for what?" he asks me.

I says, "Ready to leave it to your son." I pulled my pistol out of my belt and shoved it up almost against his forehead. You never seen such a surprised look in a man's face. His mouth dropped open, and his eyes went as big as hen eggs. He made a reach for his gun, but he never touched it. I pulled the trigger. He fell back like he had been hit with a sledgehammer.

I had caught them all by surprise, but I could see Sorrells reaching for his gun. I swung around and caught him just as he cleared leather. I watched him fall on his face in the middle of the room.

The whole place was filled with powder smoke; it was hard to see across to the far wall. But nobody else in there was any threat to me. Surely not the banker, because he raised his hands like he thought it was a holdup. Mrs. Ordway had her mouth wide open like she wanted to scream, but nothing would come out.

I says to her, "You don't have to be scared anymore. You're shed of him. What's more, you're a rich woman."

I picked up the saddlebags, swung them across my shoulder and walked out the door.

From up the street came four of Jesse Ordway's hands, walking along like they had been sent for. I was the last person they expected to see come out after the shooting. Later, when I had time to think about it, I figured they was coming down to be Ordway's "eye-witnesses" after him and Sorrells killed me.

They pulled their guns and spread out. I was about to take a shot at one of them when somebody else done it for me. I seen one of them go down and grab his leg and scream like he had gone into a fire. The others stopped in their tracks, dropped their guns and raised their hands.

There was Felipe Rios across the street, sitting on his horse. His gun was smoking like he had been burning greasewood.

I taken a look at Ordway's boy, who was trying to hold the team and keep it from running away. I says, "Boy, you better go in yonder. I think your mama needs you." Then I got on my horse, laid the saddlebags across my lap and rode over to where Felipe was.

I couldn't decide whether to thank him or raise hell with him. I says, "Thought you was going to Arlee's."

"Later," he says. "I thought you might need help."

"You can't go to Arlee's now," I tells him. "I just killed Jesse Ordway and Sorrells. They'll figure you was part of it."

He nodded like it wasn't no surprise to him. He says, "It was in your face."

"I got to leave here now," I tells him. "You feel like you can keep up with me?"

"I don't see where I have any choice," he says. "These people will hang me if I stay."

Them days when a man got in trouble he went south. A day and a half of hard riding would take us to the Rio Grande. On the other side of the river they didn't care how many *gringos* you had killed; the more the better. Felipe wasn't in very good shape for a long ride like that, but I decided he would make it if I had to tie him in the saddle.

Good sense told me we ought to ride out of that town as fast as we could make those horses go. But that was Jesse Ordway's town, and I didn't want to run. I wanted us to take our time and let them all have a good long look at our backside. We rode slow and easy down the street, past them O Bar men. One of them was still holding onto his leg and trying to make the blood stop running. I says to him, says I, "You-all are working for a widow-lady now. You better go down to the bank and see what she wants you to do."

We just walked our horses till we got past the first bend in the road, to where the brush hid us from town. I says then, "Let's ride, Felipe."

And we rode.

Chapter 2

I've come to many a fork in the road during my life, and a time or two I've took the wrong direction. One thing I've finally learned is that you never know what a woman is going to do. If I'd known more about Jesse Ordway's quiet, timid little wife, my life might of turned out a lot different. I naturally figured she would scream murder, and I didn't stay around to listen to her.

A long time later, way too late for it to do me any good, I found out she figured I'd done her a sizable favor. She told them I had killed her husband and Sorrells in self-defense. Naturally I can't exactly blame her for not telling me right then. I got away in kind of a hurry, and it taken her some time to get her thinking sorted out too, I expect. The banker, of course, told the story some different the first time, but he changed it later when he saw how the wind blew. He wasn't going to argue with a widow . . . not a *rich* widow.

Not knowing all this, and figuring they would keep

the telegraph wires hot all the way to the Rio Grande, me and Felipe kind of abused our horses in getting there. We didn't stop to rest till we was on the south side of the Bravo, drying the water out of our ears.

A man crossing the river for a day or a night's entertainment these days, he don't rightly appreciate how it was then. Going into Mexico wasn't something you done lightly or without good cause. Most of the *gringos* you found then was there because it was healthier than being someplace else, and not just because they chose it of their own free will. It was a nervous feeling to be in an alien country where they spoke a whole different language and where a man didn't know what the law was. You'll likely think that's funny, Joe Pepper worrying about obeying the law, but I always tried to. I never did hold with a man breaking the law without he had a good reason for it. I always had a good reason, or at least thought I did at the time. Once or twice, maybe, I might've erred a mite in my judgment. I was always in favor of the law as long as it didn't harm anybody.

I had a right smart of money in my saddlebags, and that was enough in itself to make a man nervous. You never know when you'll come across somebody dishonest. Some ways from the river we struck a road which Felipe said would lead us to a village ten or fifteen miles to the west. I got to thinking of all the things I'd heard about Mexican bandits and such, and of course I knowed there was many a Texas outlaw hanging out south of the Rio Grande. Them kind of people are apt to do a man harm for a lot less money than I had with me.

Along the way I kept looking around for landmarks that I would be able to remember. We came up finally to a place where the road made a bend around a motte of trees, and I thought I ought to be able to find it again. I rode on a little ways to where I didn't think Felipe would figure out the spot I had in mind, then I sent

him on ahead while I doubled back. I paced out a spot
due west of a certain forked tree and buried most of
that money wrapped up in a slicker.

I didn't distrust Felipe, exactly, it was just that I
didn't completely trust him, either. I never trusted *nobody* when it came to money, except maybe my mama
and Millie Thompson. Probably that came from a time
when I was a boy that my uncle gave me a silver dollar
for helping him chop his cotton for four days, and my
daddy taken and spent it on flour for the whole family.
That was *my* dollar, not the family's.

I kept out a little traveling money so we wouldn't
have no need to get lank or dry. After a while we came
to this village Felipe knew about. I had a few minutes'
worry as we met a bunch of soldiers guarding the road.
They stopped us and asked questions about who we
was and what we was doing there. Felipe answered for
us—told the damnedest pack of lies you ever heard.
He said later a man never wanted to tell the truth to a
bunch of soldiers because they'll hold it against you.

It was a bigger town than I had expected from what
Felipe had told me. It had growed a right smart since
he had been there as a boy. The thing I noticed right
off about it was the soldiers. You would of thought
they was fixing to have a parade, they was so many. I
never had paid any particular attention before to what
was going on in Mexico. I didn't know they had their
own war going on at the same time we was having that
unpleasantness of ours between the states. It was a
mixed-up deal. A bunch of Frenchmen had been in
there muddying up the waters, but by this time they
was out, and the Mexicans was fighting amongst theirselves over just who was supposed to be *in*. I never
could get it straight in my mind just who was against
who, because one time there would be a bunch who
was friends, and the next time the same people was
enemies and the people who had been their enemies

was their friends, and . . . well, you know how complicated life gets sometimes.

I tried not to get involved with it. I never did rightly understand what *our* war was about, so I sure didn't figure to mix into somebody else's. The longer I stayed there, though, the more I learned how hard it was to keep out of it. You couldn't stay on the fence. Somebody always had ahold of your leg, pulling to get you down.

People didn't seem to pay much attention to us when we rode in. They was used to *gringos* coming and going, and they didn't seem to get concerned about them as long as they brought money and didn't kill any of the local folks. During our War between the States there had been a good many Union sympathizers in Texas who found the climate kind of unhealthy at home and hightailed it across the river. After the war the traffic changed over . . . there was Unionists going north and a lot of unreconstructed rebels going south, swapping places with one another. The ones that went south didn't know they was just leaving one war and wading up to their necks into another one.

And besides those that was in and out of Mexico on account of the war, there was always the plain-out fugitives, looking for a place where the long arm of the law was a little short in the reach. Some of them was outlaws and killers. Some was men like me . . . good men, you know, just a little down on their luck. For all I knew, every Ranger and sheriff and two-bit *pilón* constable in Texas was out hunting for me.

I had some little advantage in knowing the language. I had been around Mexicans a fair bit over the years and could understand the lingo if they didn't take to throwing any of that educated stuff at me. I could even talk back to them in pretty good fashion, enough that I wasn't going to starve to death because I didn't know how to say "beans." First thing a man learns in another language, if he's around the people that use it, is the cusswords. Give a man a fair vocabulary of cusswords and he'll get along.

We was tired and hungry and dry to the gizzard. We sure wasn't looking for no trouble. For once, trouble wasn't looking for us, either. We hitched in front of an adobe place where we could hear a guitar player and a fiddler, and some people laughing. We knowed we wasn't getting into no church, but it sounded friendly. We ordered us a bottle of *tequila* and some supper. Barman brought us the bottle; I had to ask him for glasses. Good thing you never seen what them glasses looked like, preacher, because you'd of never drank a drop. But them days I wasn't fussy, and besides, that Mexican *tequila* was strong enough to kill anything it touched that wasn't human. Anything human too, if taken in quantity.

We ordered up something to eat. I disremember exactly what it was; I just remember that they forgot to leave the fire at the stove. That Mexican cooking took a right smart of getting used to.

Afterwards, when we was working on the second bottle, I got to noticing how many *gringo* faces was coming in and going out. First thought I had was that some was probably spies for the Rangers and the other laws, but then I decided the hell with them, let them spy. As long as I didn't cross that river, I doubted they would come and get me. After I had studied on it a while, I decided most of the people was like me, they couldn't go back. Or wouldn't.

As Mexican towns went, it was a comfortable sort of a place. They didn't ask questions as long as you paid cash. Me and Felipe, we decided it was a good place to stay and rest awhile. His leg was still causing him a right smart of trouble. I hadn't made any plans as to what to do with myself. I had always thought I would enjoy just laying around someplace with nothing to do but play cards and drink whiskey and eat. I did, too, for the first few days. After that the days got to running forty-eight hours long. I was still young then. I hadn't learned patience.

In the back of my mind I had thought I would just sort of kill time there till I figured the law had put my case back in the warming oven, then I would dig up my money, cross the river and make my way west, maybe to Arizona or California. I sure didn't figure on setting down roots in Mexico. So we just laid around days, and nights we'd work our way from one *cantina* to another, trying to find one that had better liquor. None of them did, but the hunting gave us something to do.

I got to noticing how many *gringos* had taken up business of one sort or another, like *cantinas* and mercantile and that kind of thing. It began crossing my mind that maybe I ought to do the same. But I didn't know nothing about the mercantile trade, and all I knowed then about the saloon business was what I had learned from the front side of the bar, which is a damn bad place to learn anything.

Gradually I came to know that some of the boys wasn't completely idle. One time there was half a dozen *gringos* whose acquaintance I had made that disappeared from sight for several days. They showed up again, finally, spending money like it was seawater and they was drunken sailors, scooping it out with both hands. Word filtered down about a big bank robbery in one of the Texas towns a ways up from the border. I played poker with some of them boys and won a fair part of their take and noticed a little bloodstain on some of the bills. Didn't seem to have no trouble cashing them at the bar, though. They was all negotiable.

I could've went with them boys on their little "trips" if I had of wanted to, but that wasn't my style of work. Being handy with the pasteboards, I could always get a good part of their money anyway without having to travel any farther than the gaming tables. That was

safer than comparing marksmanship with some sharp-
eyed Ranger, too.

By and by I got to feeling real restless, cooped up
in town like I was, and sometimes I would take my
good gray Tennessee horse and ride out over the country, just looking at it. Seemed to me like it ought to be
good for ranching. There was some Mexican outfits,
mostly owned by the big old rich *hacendados*, and
some few that was owned by *gringos*. The way I was
told, the best way for a *gringo* to operate was to take
in some local Mexican as a partner. That made the deal
set better with the other Mexicans, and they wasn't so
apt to steal him blind. I had noticed a lot the same in
regard to *gringos* who was in business in town. The
most successful was the ones that had Mexican partners.

Looking at that land and the cattle on it made me
start feeling a little homesick, which is a dangerous
thing for a man on the dodge. It gets to giving him
foolish notions about going back. I must of said something to somebody, when I was feeling the *tequila* a
little, though I never could remember it afterwards. If
I hadn't, that Orville Jackson never would of latched
onto me.

Later on I figured it wasn't just chance that put Jackson into a poker game with me. But at the time it
seemed like a natural thing that we sort of fell together.
I figured from the first that he was on the up-and-up
because his last name wasn't Smith, and his first name
wasn't Bill or Jim. I figured nobody would just make
up a name like Orville.

The way Jackson told it, he had been in business in
Texas before the war, and his favor kind of stayed attached to the Union. After the war broke out, there was
some people who felt so strong about it that they made
it their business to roam around the countryside hanging Unionists, or people they thought might even have
any inclinations toward the Union. Them same people

are the kind that take prisoners out of the jail at night and lynch them but never have the guts to join a posse that goes out and catches them in the first place. They get real righteous, but they only kill when there ain't no danger in it.

Anyway, this Orville Jackson sold his property in something of a hurry and lit out for Mexico between two days.

Some of the Unionists who went to Mexico found ways to get to the North and fight us rebel boys, but Jackson didn't have that strong a feeling about the war. He looked around awhile and bought him some land in Mexico and built himself a ranch. He taken in a Mexican partner, naturally, and all in all he done right well for a *gringo*. But lately the partner had died and there was a lot the partner's widow didn't understand about the ranch business. With the war long since over, Jackson was kind of thinking he would like to sell his ranch and go back to Texas. He figured by now them old hanging parties was probably busy licking the boots of the Yankee occupation soldiers and selling them hay and oats and horses and whiskey and getting rich off of the Union. Which was correct, of course; that was exactly what they was doing. Them kind of people was always changeable in their politics.

Jackson didn't proposition me right off to buy the place. I hadn't given him no reason that I remembered to think I had the money to buy it with. But he had figured from looking at me that I knowed cows. Once a man gets cow manure stuck to the bottom of his boots, it don't ever all come off. We talked about cattle a right smart, and I told him about me going up the trail to Kansas. So he asked me if I would like to go out and spend a few days at the ranch with him and help him with the branding. He said he would pay me for my time.

I figured I would make a lot more money at the gaming tables, but I was hungry to get back out in the country for a change. I told him I would go if we could take Felipe with us. He didn't see nothing wrong with that.

The morning we started out, things got a little excited in town for a while. We run into an agitated bunch of the local citizens, running up toward the local *calabozo*. They sort of swept us along. We got there in time to see the soldiers bring out a bunch of men— maybe seven or eight, including a couple that couldn't of been more than just boys—and stand them up against an adobe wall. The people was yelling and cursing and begging, but the officer in charge seemed like a man who enjoyed his work. He lined up a firing squad and raised his sword and called off the signals.

Now, I've seen men die in battle more times than once, and I've seen them die other places. But I had never seen a firing squad before. Most everybody I had ever seen fall had a gun in his hand. Watching the soldiers stand them poor devils up there helpless and shoot them down like cattle at the slaughter . . . well, I tell you, my blood ran cold. It took half a bottle of *tequila* to burn the chill out of me.

Jackson didn't enjoy it either, but he said it was something a man had to pretend like he didn't see. Happened down there all the time, and a *gringo* just had to keep from taking sides or getting himself involved. Pretty soon he was talking about cattle again, but I kept seeing them people slammed back against that adobe wall with their blood leaking out.

We was half the day getting there. It wasn't nothing fancy, Jackson's place, just a kind of adobe headquarters and brush pens and the like. His wife that he had brought from Texas had died on him a good while back, and he was living with a good-looking Mexican woman. At this time he still hadn't made any move toward selling me the ranch, but I had already begun thinking about it. I got to wondering if he would throw that woman in on the deal if a man was to buy him out.

Don't look so shocked, preacher. My wife Millie had been dead for quite a while by that time. I had got to where I was watching them girls around the *cantinas* some, and they was looking better to me all the time. I don't suppose a man in your line of work ever gets them feelings, but a man in mine is subject to a lapse now and again, like the fever and the ague. I've found that the best cure for temptation is generally to give in to it, get it over with, and then you can turn your mind to other things. Long as you resist, it keeps coming back at you and getting in the way of your thinking.

As you get up toward the age where I'm at now, of course, it don't bother you much. You get a lot more of the fever and the ague.

Later on, remembering back, I come to realize that Jackson must of sniffed it out somehow that I had money, the same way he recognized that I knowed the cow. He didn't really need no help from me for the branding; he had more good Mexican *vaqueros* than he needed. Mostly he just kept me with him and showed me the good points about the place. He had that good-looking woman bringing us something to drink every time we was in the house. He didn't have to be very smart to figure out that I enjoyed watching her go by.

I had been there three days before he throwed the question at me. We was sitting in the house that night, sipping at some good American whiskey. "What do you think of it?" he asks me. The woman was walking away from us at the time. I told him I thought she looked mighty good. He let me know he was talking about the ranch, not about the woman. And he let me know the whole deal was for sale. Including the woman.

I remembered about his Mexican partner, and that there was a widow. He said the partner was a partner on paper only, just for the satisfaction of local politics, and that the widow didn't own but a token share.

Not knowing the widow, I had my doubts. I was afraid she might not be happy with the deal. She could get me crossways with her countrymen and give me hell.

"But you *know* the widow," Jackson says, "and what's more, she likes you." He pointed with his chin toward the kitchen. "María there, she's my partner's widow."

After that he didn't have too hard a job selling me on the notion. His proposition sounded real good. Too good, in fact. I was suspicious of it at first. Nobody ever gives you anything in this life without they're trying to take something even bigger away from you. Bad as I wanted to, I couldn't see my way clear; the deal just sounded too good. But by and by I caught him lying about his calf crop. I had already seen enough of his tally books to know he couldn't have as many calves as he claimed.

Once I caught him trying to cheat me I felt better. If you can't find out where a man is trying to best you on a trade, you'd better steer clear of it.

The upshot was that we finally made a deal. I slipped off by myself, rode to where I had buried that money and dug it up.

I reckon I kind of expected Jackson to be a little sentimental about leaving the place after all of them years, but he must not of been. Or else it hurt him so much that he didn't want to stretch things out. We signed the papers in front of a magistrate in town, and he lit right out for the Rio Grande.

Felipe was my *majordomo*, sort of, though at first we had to leave things to the regular *vaqueros*, pretty much. They knowed the country, whereas me and Felipe had a lot to learn.

I hadn't been there more than two weeks before I learned why Orville Jackson had wanted to sell. There was some four-legged wolves killing on the baby calves and some two-legged ones stealing on the grown cattle. A man could poison the four-legged ones, but the two-legged variety was a whole different proposition. I found out they was mainly of two varieties— the government soldiers on the one side and the local rebels on the other.

The one thing Orville Jackson had neglected to tell me was that he was serving as a sort of free commissary to both sides of the war.

In Texas there was always one quick and final remedy in a situation like this. If you caught a man stealing off of you, and you got the drop on him, you reformed him real quick. That way he didn't ever come back and trouble you again unless you was subject to bad dreams, which I never was. But this here was a lot more ticklish proposition. María pointed out to me that if I was to kill any soldiers they'd have me in front of that same adobe wall where I seen them citizens lined up. If I was to kill any of the citizens . . . well, all the adobe walls wasn't in town.

She said the best thing for me to do was to just accept that which couldn't be changed and go on the best I could. Keep the cows happy by putting out plenty of bulls on the range, she said, and hope they kept the calves coming faster than the thieves could steal them. I could pretty soon see it wasn't that easy. I was always a slow reader, but I'm apt with figures. I could tell without counting on my fingers that they was getting way ahead of me. Orville Jackson had left Mexico just in time.

Things really started closing in on me one day when I was up on the part of the ranch that fronted along the river. In a way that was my favorite part, and in another I hated it. I would go up to that river and look across and get to wanting so bad to go back to Texas that I couldn't hardly keep from spurring out into the water. But sometimes I could see people over there. I was satisfied in my own mind that they was all Rangers and sheriffs, camping over there waiting for me to do something foolish.

That particular day me and Felipe heard a sudden lot of shooting a mile or so upriver. Felipe's inclination was to head off in the opposite direction, which would of been smart, but I thought it was somebody killing my cattle. I told Felipe in a sharp way to come on and go with me. I didn't know exactly what I was going to do about it when I got there, but I figured it would come to me in due course. I generally found that when the time came, the idea came, too.

Felipe sure wasn't keen on it, which led me to wonder if maybe he didn't know more of what was going on than I did. We loped over a hill and seen a big clearing down there leading away from the river. There was maybe half a dozen men, dead and dying, scattered over that clearing, and some horses and packmules with them. We seen one man still laying down behind a packmule, firing a shot now and again at somebody over in the brush. By and by he ran out of ammunition. I seen some soldiers get up from that brush and walk out toward him. They was evidently hollering at each other, but me and Felipe was too far away to hear any of it. The man stood up with his hands in the air, and some more soldiers came out of the brush. There was one with them wearing a bright-colored uniform, and I knew right off he was an officer of some kind. He was giving orders. The soldiers scattered out, checking all the dead and wounded men and animals. The officer walked up to that prisoner, talked to him a minute, then pulled out a pistol and shot him in the head.

He hollered something at the soldiers, and they shot two more men that was only wounded, so that they wasn't just wounded anymore.

"Let's go," says Felipe. "It isn't healthy here."

Right about then they spotted us. I began to feel like Felipe was smarter than I used to give him credit for. I wished he had been a better persuader. The officer

pointed in our direction, and I knowed it was too late
to run. Some of the soldiers spurred up to us.

The only thing left for us to do was to stand our
ground and try to talk ourselves out of trouble, seeing
as it wasn't none of our business to start with. It wasn't
none of mine, anyway, but I could tell right off that
Felipe considered it his. While he waited he cussed the
soldiers and called them a lot of things that didn't fit
comfortable on the ear. I had taken great pains not to
choose up sides, but being of the blood, I reckon Felipe
couldn't help it. He might as easy of taken the other
side, but he didn't.

I don't suppose you ever had occasion to look at the
business end of a dozen rifles, preacher, I tell you, the
muzzle looks as big around as a number-four washtub.
Them soldiers invited us to go down with them for a
conference with the *capitán*, and we accepted the invitation.

When we got down into the clearing I could tell real
easy what the excitement was about. They had taken
the packs off of them dead mules, and they was full of
rifles and ammunition. Them citizens they had ambushed had just swum across the river from the Texas
side with a bunch of U.S. Army goods for the rebels.
Now, I'm sure the U.S. Army hadn't *given* them all
that weaponry. There was a bunch of them unreconstructed Confederates on the Texas side, though, that
would cheerfully burglarize an armory and sell for gold
to any and all comers.

I couldn't figure out at first why they had tried to
cross the Rio Grande in the daylight instead of in the
dark. Then I noticed one civilian amongst the soldiers
and seen the *capitán* give him a handful of silver. It
didn't take even a *gringo* long to figure out that these
boys had been betrayed. The betrayer didn't wait
around to count his money; he acted like he had a
whole hive of bees in his britches.

I seen the way Felipe looked at him. I figured if we

got out of this mess with our skin still on tight, and
Felipe ever crossed trails with that Judas, there was
going to be a little knifework done.

The *capitán* taken his slow, sweet time in getting
around to us. He was like a cat playing with a mouse
that ain't ever really going to go nowhere. He just gave
Felipe a glance, but he stared at me a long time like a
man who enjoys his work. "A *gringo*," he says, real
pleased with himself. "I am Captain Tiburcio Santos.
You would be, I believe, the Señor Peeler."

I told him he sure was right, that I was Joe Peeler.
That was my real name, you remember.

He had a grin wider than the wave on a slop jar,
only it wasn't at all funny. "And what reason, Señor
Peeler, can you think of why we should not shoot you
right here and leave you lying dead among your
friends?"

Well, sir, I could think of a hundred good reasons,
and ninety-nine of them was that I was too young to
die. I didn't think that would impress him much, so I
told him the other one. "Because these was no friends
of mine. I never seen them in my whole life till just
now."

He says, "I find that hard to believe. Convince me."

I didn't waste no time in the telling, how come me and
Felipe to be here, how we had heard the shooting
and had come to investigate because this was my ranch,
and because I figured anything which happened on it
was of more than just passing interest to me. I told him
these citizens—whoever they was—was trespassers on
private land.

Pretty soon I got to feeling like he knowed it all the
time, that he was just playing with me because he liked
to watch me sweat. And I was doing plenty of that.
There was a sergeant sitting on his horse beside the
captain, and he had his pistol pointed straight at me,
and his finger was twitching. All he was waiting for
was the word.

The captain said he thought it would be natural for me—being the owner of the land—to take a bribe or a *mordida* to let these louse-ridden, dirty rebels smuggle arms across it to fight against the freedom-loving, legally constituted authorities. I had to keep telling him that I wasn't in no way mixed up in their Mexican politics, that I was a peaceful, law-abiding man who had just bought this place and was trying in my own awkward way to make a decent living out of it.

It gradually soaked in on me that if I had really been part of the smuggling setup, he'd of known it through the Judas. He was just fishing around for a payoff. The *mordida* is a kind of a hidden tax that everybody pays. A little man pays a little *mordida* to a little official for little favors. A big man pays a big *mordida* to a big official for big favors. For me and Felipe to ride away from here without any surplus holes in us was going to be considered a big favor.

It never was in my nature to bow and scrape and make myself little, not unless it was for a good cause. This was for a good cause.

I tells that captain, "I'm sorry if you or any of your men have come to any danger or harm on my land. And although I am in no way responsible for this, I would be glad to have you-all take a few steers back to town with you for the benefit of all your company."

The captain said he could take *all* the cattle and leave me and Felipe dead, if that was his inclination. I told him I realized he could but hoped he would see fit to take the gift as my guest . . . my *honored* guest. I damn near gagged.

The captain sprung his trap then. He says, "I had some conversations with the previous owner of this ranch and thought I had completed an arrangement with him. Now I must start over with you. It appears to me that what you need is a Mexican partner."

I told him I already had a Mexican partner.

"A woman." He kind of snickered. "I know all about

that. What you need is a *strong* partner, one who has influence in the right places. One who has power at his command. One who someday will perhaps even be governor, *quién sabe*? In the right hands this property of yours could become a highway of commerce with those on the other side of the river."

I knowed what he meant by that. It would be a handy place to bring cattle stolen from the Texas side of the Rio Grande. That thought had already occurred to me.

I knowed then why he hadn't already shot me.

I says, "I'll have to think about it some." The longer he gave me to think about it, the longer my health would hold up.

He says, "You think, but be sure you think right. A partner in the right position could make you a wealthy man. An enemy in the right position could bring you ruin . . . and death. So think about it, Señor Peeler, until we meet each other again."

I couldn't decide right then who I was the maddest at, him or Orville Jackson. That was why Jackson had wanted to unload this place on me; he was fixing to get himself a new Mexican partner that wouldn't fit in his bed. Now Jackson was on the right side of the river, singing happy songs to himself and counting my money, and here I sat face to face with a brazen thief who was about to clean my plow.

The soldiers gathered up all the arms and ammunition including me and Felipe's guns. After they was out of earshot, Felipe commenced calling them bloody butchers and swine and such other endearments. I told him none of this was our fight and we'd better stay out of it. Didn't seem like he heard me, and anyway, we *was* mixed up in it already. I told him finally that it might be a cagy move on our part if we was to put the spurs to our horses and leave this locality. If any of them rebel citizens was to come along and find us here amongst their dead friends and kin, they might get the wrong idea and do us bodily harm.

Felipe understood those citizens pretty good. We left there in a lope, him taking the lead.

María was some upset when we told her that night. She seemed to be more sorely afflicted by the fact that the packtrain got ambushed than she was over me and Felipe having ourselves a narrow escape. By and by I found myself sitting at the table all alone. I got up and went to the kitchen for a cup of coffee and found María and Felipe in a real serious discussion. I pulled back so they wouldn't see me. My first thought was that Felipe was getting some partnership rights that I hadn't intended to give him. Directly I seen him and her go out together to one of the brush *jacales* where the *vaqueros* stayed. They talked to the *vaqueros* a while. Finally one of them went to the barn, saddled a horse and rode off in the night.

It gradually came to me that there was a lot more to María than Jackson had told me. Probably more than he knowed.

I can't say I ever entertained any real hopes of getting to be a big cowman in Mexico, but in my idle moments I sometimes let myself dream a little. It was the kind of dream some of them Mexican boys get from smoking that funny weed in their cigarettes. But it's a hard go being a cowman. Even when everything goes right, it's hard to make ends meet. And when you're trying to operate in a country where they're fighting a war across your land, and the only time they ever stop is to go fill up their bellies on your beef, well sir, you *have* got complications. They didn't just pick the big steers to butcher. Times I'd come across a calf bawling for milk and would find its mammy laying there with both of her hind quarters gone. A man can afford to lose the steers sometimes, but the cow is the factory.

I'd come in at night cussing about it, and María would always take the rebels' part.

"They are fighting for what is good and just," she would always say.

They probably thought they was. But I've watched
them kinds of fights off and on for a good many years,
and it always seems like somebody gets at the head of
it sooner or later and turns everybody else's dying into
a personal gain for himself. You show me a hero,
preacher, and I'll show you a damn fool who is being
used for somebody else's profit.

I would get so mad at María that I would almost put
her out of the house. But never quite. I had a notion
that she would find all the sympathy she needed from
Felipe.

I quit going to town unless I was forced to it, and then
I would try to go in at night, do whatever I had to and get
out. Sooner or later I knowed I was going to have to face
that Captain Santos again, and I wanted to put it off as
long as I could. If he made up his mind to declare himself in as my partner, I knowed I would have a hard time
stopping him. He had the whole local military contin-
gent to back him up, and all I had was a little bunch
of *vaqueros* that didn't really owe me anything.

Of course I could do what I had done to Jesse Ordway; I could just shoot him. But I wouldn't live to see
the sunrise.

I wasn't sure this Mexico ranch was worth dying for.
Not *me* dying for, anyway.

Did you ever get yourself into a mess of fleas, to
where you didn't know which spot to scratch first?
Where you itched in a dozen places and had only two
hands to scratch with?

That was the shape they had me in. I'd find out
somebody was running off cattle on the south end of
the place, and I'd ride down there as fast as I could
go. While I was gone, some more would hit the north
end. Sometimes it was the rebels, sometimes the soldiers from town. I can't say they was overgreedy; they
just taken a few here and a few there. But you can

finally empty a well with a teacup if you dip fast
enough.

The whole thing come to a head one day just by
pure luck . . . *bad* luck, as it turned out. I heard some
cows bawling and rode up on a bunch of them rebel
citizens driving off twelve or fifteen head. They was
taking the cows and trying to leave the calves behind
so they could travel faster. If you know anything about
cattle you know it ain't in an old cow's nature to go
off and leave her calf behind without she puts up a
devil of a struggle over it.

I don't know what I figured I could do about it,
seeing as they had me pretty badly outnumbered, but I
was so mad I rode down there anyway. I wasn't so
mad as to be stupid, though. I didn't put my gun on
them. A couple or three had their guns on *me*. There
was seven or eight of them, a lot of people for such a
small bunch of cattle.

I picked out the one I figured was the leader. I told
him in the nicest way I knowed how that I considered
him a lowdown sneak thief and a cross between a rattlesnake and a coyote. He was a fiery-eyed young gent
of about Felipe's general size and age. I never thought
about it then, but later I got to wondering if they might
of been kin, seeing as Felipe had taken to such strong
feelings about the rebels. That *hombre* just sat there
and looked at me while I talked to him. His eyes
crackled like dry brush on fire. When I had run down
a little, he set in on me.

"These cattle are of Mexico," he says, "and you are
a *gringo*. By what right do you claim cattle in Mexico?"

"By right of money," I says. "I bought these cattle
and this ranch fair and square with good old American
green-back money." I've never been noplace in my life
where money didn't talk louder than the law, if there
was enough of it.

"Stolen money, no doubt," says he. "Or money made

from the sweat and blood of poor Mexicans you *Tejanos* have enslaved."

Me, I never had enslaved nobody, black, white or brown, and I damn well told him so. But you ought to know how them fanatic types are, preacher, since the worst fanatics in the world are in the field of religion. They don't hear nothing except their own voices, and they think it's the voice of God.

He gave me a lecture on heaven and hell and the rights of the down-trodden and the greed of the rich, and all that. Later on, when I was in a better mood to ponder on it, I almost laughed. Why, he considered me *rich*. I reckon a man with a patched shirt looks rich to the one that's got no shirt atall.

Since he seen fit to bring religion into it, I tried to give him a lecture about that commandment which says "Thou shalt not steal." He acted like he thought I was trying to change the subject on him. He didn't see it as stealing to take something off of a rich *gringo*, especially when it was going to feed the poor and the rebellious.

It was pretty much of a standoff. I wasn't going to convince him, and it would've been suicidal to of tried to shoot him. I should of gone off and left them in possession, but that went against all my training. So I stayed and argued with them whilst they kept on driving my cattle away. I was just wasting my time. I wasn't any more to them than a gnat buzzing around a horse's rump.

Turned out that I stayed a little too long. All of a sudden there was the biggest bunch of shooting you ever heard, and bullets flying around and horses squealing and pitching. For a minute I thought maybe it was a bunch of my *vaqueros* come to my rescue, but I disabused myself of that notion when I seen the uniforms. It was the soldiers, ambushing this bunch of cow-stealing rebels.

I can't say a lot for their marksmanship, because

most of the rebels got clean away. They rode like they was all married men, getting back to the bosom of their families. I decided it might be smart if I went home too. But I didn't get very far. One of them soldiers got off a lucky shot, and that was the end of my good old Tennessee gray horse that I had brought home from the big war I ate a bucketful of pure old Mexican dirt and had a little trouble getting my breath started again. Time I was able to get on my feet, there didn't seem to be much use in it. A bunch of them soldiers had me surrounded, and it was like it had been that day me and Felipe stumbled onto the ambush of the gunrunners.

Captain Santos wasn't with them this time, which I thought at first was some improvement. But his sergeant was there, the one with the itchy trigger finger. I figured I'd try to put the best face on a bad situation. I thanked him for rescuing me from that bunch of cattle thieves.

You know something? He didn't believe a bit of that.

One of the men tickled me in the ribs with the muzzle of his rifle. The sergeant motioned for me to get to my feet, *pronto*. I didn't see where it would help my situation to argue with him. They searched me and taken away the pistol I had on. That was the second time they had taken guns away from me. Seemed like they was determined not only to make me feed their army but to equip it with artillery. One of the men taken my pocketwatch, the one with Millie's picture in the back. I grabbed at it and got a gunbutt up beside my head. I ate another bucketful of dirt.

When my eyes cleared to where I could see, that sergeant had my watch open, listening to the little tune it played and looking at Millie's picture. He made some comment about her that I'd of been pleased to kill a man for if the circumstances had been more favorable. But I was at a considerable disadvantage at the time. I could feel the blood running down the side of my face, hot and sticky. I had a headache that would of set a mule on its haunches.

"This time," the sergeant says, "we have caught you redhanded, *gringo*, working with those damned rebels."

I had already argued myself out, trying to make that rebel see my side of it. I didn't have it left in me to argue with this sergeant. I expected them to shoot me right where I sat. I hurt so bad that it would of been merciful. But mercy didn't have no part in his thinking.

"*El capitán* will be most pleased to see you, *gringo*," says he. "Especially when I tell him the company you keep."

I don't suppose you ever had your head cracked with a gunbutt? It makes it awful hard to concentrate. Just getting on the horse was a chore. Mine was dead, but they brought up one which a rebel wasn't going to need anymore. I couldn't tell what color it was, hardly. I fell off once. The sergeant tied a short piece of rope around my neck and the other end to the saddlehorn, and told me that the next time I fell off I would hang myself. That helped my concentration some.

It was way after dark when we finally got into town. The fiddles and the guitars was playing in the *cantinas*, but I didn't enjoy the music. They drug me through some big tall wooden doors into a *patio* of some kind, and across to a cell which had a wooden door that must of weighed five hundred pounds. They throwed me in there and locked the door and left.

I laid there a long time waiting for my head to quit hurting, but it never did. It was too dark to see anything, so I asked if there was anybody with me, and I found out I had the whole thing to myself. I felt around and found a goatskin, which was all the bed they provided. The way I felt right then, a feather tick wouldn't of helped. I can't say I slept much. My head hurt like thunder, and I found out I wasn't as alone in that cell as I thought I was. Little crawling and running things was in there with me. They must of liked the place because they didn't seem to be making any great effort to get out. They was just trying to be friendly, especially the lice.

There wasn't no window in the cell, but come morning I could see light start to seep around the edges of that heavy wooden door. The walls was of adobe. It appeared to me I could probably cut my way through them if I had plenty of time and something to scratch with. But that could turn into a lifetime proposition. Walls like that was often three feet thick. And when a man got through one, chances was he would find himself in another cell like the one he had crawled out of. I doubted they figured on keeping me around long enough for me to find out.

They didn't seem to figure I needed any breakfast; leastways they neglected to bring it. My head hurt me a lot worse than my stomach did, anyway. I'd been looking at the daylight around that door for a long time before finally I heard somebody thumping around out there, fiddling with the bolt. The light hurt my eyes when they swung the door in, but I got used to it in a minute. There stood that sergeant with a mean black whip in his hand, and right behind him was Captain Santos.

"Señor Peeler," Santos says, kind of smug and satisfied with himself, "I hope you slept well."

Now, that rankled me a little because I knowed he didn't care whether I'd got any sleep or not. I changed the subject considerable and tried to give him some idea what kind of a son of a bitch—pardon me, preacher—I thought he really was. The sergeant commenced a little persuasion with the whip.

It was the first time anybody had taken a whip to me in my life, if you don't count the times my daddy taken a quirt to my rosy little cheeks when I was a button. This wasn't no quirt, it was one of them old blacksnakes like they use down there to drive bulls into the ring. It had a bite like something out of hell. I rolled over to get away from it, bumped my sore head on the hard dirt floor and come near fainting.

I heard the captain say, "Enough, Sergeant. I think he understands you."

I understood *both* of them. I had very little hope right then that I would ever get out of that place alive.

The captain says, "So this time you were caught, Señor Peeler, helping those people drive away cattle to feed their accursed rebel camps."

I thought I ought to tell him once, whether he believed me or not, so I says, "I caught them taking my cattle. I was trying to stop them." I was wasting my breath, and there wasn't much of it to spare.

The captain says, "Why weren't they dead, then, some of them? And why aren't *you* dead? If you had really tried to stop them you would have killed some of them, and they would have killed you. You lie, *gringo*. Sergeant, show him what we think of *gringos* who lie to us."

There was nothing I could do but curl up in a ball and take it, and try to think up all the slow and brutal ways I could kill them both, if ever I got the chance. With all due respect to your profession, preacher, these sky pilots that get up and preach against hate don't know what they're talking about. They don't know how good it can make a man feel to hate under the right circumstances. I've knowed times when hate was all that kept a man alive.

The sergeant finally quit whipping me. Santos says, "Are you ready to admit your guilt?"

I gave him some advice, which he didn't take, and the sergeant whipped me again. Then he left, and it was just me and the captain in there by ourselves. I figured up my chances of killing him before the rest of them could kill me. They wasn't much good. I was so weak I probably couldn't of made his nose bleed. He must of read my mind, because he reminded me that he had a whole squad of men just outside the door, and they would leave me looking like a milk strainer if I made one wrong move.

"I am sorry about this," says he. "I looked forward to being a partner with you."

"Go to hell," says I.

That didn't seem to bother him much this time. The shape he had me in, I can see why he was getting more tolerant. He says, "No, we can't be partners anymore. I am going to buy you out."

That sounded a little strange to me, him talking about *buying*. Looked to me like all he had to do was *take*.

I told him I wasn't selling, but he told me I would; it was just a question of *when*. He asked me if I was hungry. I told him I was. He said that sure was too bad, because I wouldn't get nothing to eat until I decided to sell out, or until there was snow three feet deep out there in the *patio*. And that wasn't no snow country.

The steel bolt sounded like a gunshot when they locked that door shut on me again and left me in there with the rats and the cockroaches and the lice. Off and on all day I could hear people shuffling around outside, but that door never opened again. Finally I watched the light fade from around it and knowed it was nighttime. That goatskin felt a little better; I slept a right smart. My head quit hurting, but my stomach got to raising Cain with me. I had done without anything to eat a good many times before, but I never had got to where I could get along without noticing it like some people seem to. I'd rather face up to a posse of deputy sheriffs than to put up with an empty stomach.

The light gradually come around the door again, so I knowed it was daytime. I got to listening for them to come, but they didn't. I drawed up my belt as tight as I could. People tell you that'll help, but I'm here to inform you otherwise. There's no substitute for a square meal.

I judged it was along about the middle of the day before finally I heard them working that bolt. I shut my eyes, because the light was going to hurt. The captain came in, him and the sergeant. The sergeant was carrying his old friend the blacksnake. My back was all sore and welted from the treatment he had already given me. I could feel my flesh crawl when I looked at that whip.

Santos had some papers in his hand. Says he, "I have been to a lawyer, and he has drawn up these papers for me." He handed me something all written out in a nice hand, and punched with a fancy seal. It was all in Mexican. I could talk Mexican fair to middling and understand it when they talked, but I couldn't read their writing much. I handed it back to him and told him I didn't know what it was. He said it was a deed to the ranch. He reached in his shirt and pulled out a little leather bag with a puckerstring drawed up tight. He shook it so I could hear the rattle of coin.

"Gold," says he. "This gold and your freedom when you sign this deed."

For a minute I was sore tempted. I says, "And how about something to eat?"

"When you sign," says he.

I had no way to know how much gold he had in that sack. It probably wasn't nowhere near what I had paid Orville Jackson, but right then I was a whole lot more concerned with getting away than I was with the money. I was on the point of telling him yes when my thinking got to running a little straighter. All of a sudden it come to me that once he had my name on that paper, he could do anything he wanted to with me. He could kill me and take that gold back. If I was in his place, that's what I would of done.

If I signed that paper I was a dead man.

I never was one to beat around the bush, so I told

him just the way my mind was running. It made him mad that I could see through him, I reckon, because he said something sharp to the sergeant and walked out. The sergeant went to work on me with that whip to where I quit worrying about my empty stomach.

That was the last I seen of them that day. Night come, and I sat there all huddled up on the goatskin doing a lot of thinking. Two whole days and a bit of another they had had me in there without a thing to eat. You can't imagine how one of them tight little cells gets to smelling, either, especially when nature calls and you got noplace else to go. I tell you, I was sure down in my thinking.

I didn't know how things went by Mexican law, but I knowed by American law I didn't have no legal right to sign away the whole ranch, just my own share in the partnership. Exactly how much of a share María owned had never been straight in my mind; it was maybe ten percent, or something like that—whatever her husband had to make it look right to the Mexicans. That was a technicality, and I never was no hand at technicalities.

One thing bothered me. If all they needed was my signature, why didn't they just forge it? Then they could shoot me and drag me off to the buzzards. I sure wasn't going to raise up from the dead and contest them. I wondered, but I had sense enough not to ask them; maybe they just hadn't thought of it.

Gradually I realized that in the end Santos was going to get my signature. But the longer I could hold it away from him the more chance I had to see another sunrise. When you're that close to the taw line, you realize that even living in a dark smelly cell is better than dying.

They didn't wait till noon the next time; they was there early, Santos and the sergeant, and a detail of men that stayed outside.

Under ordinary circumstances when you get into a negotiation in Mexico you'll find it takes a long time.

They'll visit and talk about everything but the business at hand. When it finally comes into the conversation it's real casual, like something that just popped into their minds that minute and ain't important anyway.

Santos wasn't like that. Right off he says, "You ready to sign?"

I asks him, "How much gold you got in that sack?"

He says it don't matter, it's more than I deserve. I says, "I want more, a lot more." The sergeant moved up with his whip, but the captain says, "*Bueno*, you can have more."

Says I, "You fill that sack to where you can't cram no more into it and still draw the string tight."

The captain said all right, he would. No argument. Right then I knowed all my suspicions was right. He would pay me anything he had to because he was going to take it back off of my dead body anyway. Same as Jesse Ordway had figured. From his standpoint a man couldn't hardly beat a deal like that.

Santos waved the deed at me.

My hand was shaking, I was so weak from not having anything to eat. I told him I couldn't write my name in that kind of shape, that I was in bad need of nourishment. And I told him I couldn't eat it here in this place because it smelled so bad.

He thought he had me beat, so all of a sudden there wasn't nothing too good for me. He says to come on, he'll take me to his quarters and have some food brought to me. He led me out of that cell, and I made up my mind right then and there that I wasn't ever going back into it. I still held a few cards in my hand. I was going to play them out one at a time and as careful as I could.

Walking was a chore at first. I had been sitting or laying down in that cell for most of three days and hadn't gotten to exercise my legs.

I doubt that they fed their other condemned men as well as they fed me, but of course they wasn't trying to get as much from them. I had me some *tortillas* and some eggs and *cabrito* and black coffee, and I topped it all off with a long drink of *tequila*, which was of a pretty fair grade. He was a captain and could afford better than most of the *peons* and the convict soldiers. I had eaten till I had filled out every wrinkle in my belly and even hurt a little bit.

I always agreed with the Indians on one point: when you can eat, *eat!* You can't ever be sure when your next meal is coming.

A couple of good-looking young women cleared off the table. The captain pinched one of them twice, fore and aft. He was feeling pretty good about then. He had had a little snort of *tequila* himself. She slapped his hand, kind of gentle. I figured she was one woman whose work was never done.

The captain brought out the deed again, and he says, "Is your hand steady enough now to sign?"

I had played one card and got my belly filled. Now I played me another. I says, "In my own good time, Captain. You promised to fill up that sack with gold."

He walked over to the bed and got down on his knees and pulled out a strongbox. It had a Texas bank name on it, and I could well imagine how he come into possession. It had a padlock that could of been used for a leg iron. When he swung the lid open, he taken a big canvas bag out and opened it to get some more coins. Soon as I seen their gold color my natural ambition came to the front. I says, "That's all right, just let me have the whole bag."

He chided me some about the sin of greed, but I didn't figure he qualified as no preacher. Finally he brought that whole canvas bag over and laid it on the table. Oh, but it had a fine solid sound to it. The ring of gold and silver pieces was always my favorite kind of music.

"Now," he says, "sign."

I picked up the bags one at a time, the little leather

one first and then the big canvas sack. I had no way
of knowing how much real money they held, but I sure
liked the heft of them. The liking must of showed, and
he thought he had set the hook for sure. He pushed the
deed in my face.

Says I, "*Capitán*, it occurs to me that when I sign
this deed you'll have all you want from me. You could
take me out to that adobe wall and be shed of me good
and proper. You'd have all this gold back and my ranch
besides. I wouldn't be very smart to get into that
shape."

The sergeant stepped up and volunteered to wear a
little more shine off of that blacksnake. For a minute
it looked like the captain was fixing to let him; his face
went as dark as old shoe leather. Him and the sergeant
went off in a corner and had theirselves a whispering
conference. Directly the captain came back. He says in
a hard voice, "Just what is it you want?"

I told him I wanted to go to the Rio Grande.

He drawed his pistol and cocked it and shoved it in
my face. "*Gringo*," says he, "I would not have to take
you to the wall. I could shoot you right here and splat-
ter your brains all over this floor. I could have your
carcass dragged off to the brush like a mongrel dog."

He didn't have to tell me that; I already knowed it.
Says I, "That's why I want to be safe at the river before
I sign."

He cussed me for a double-crossing hound who had
eaten his food and drunk his *tequila*, then refused to
honor my word. I told him he still had my word. I
would sign the deed. But I would do it when I was
safe at the river. Signing it now, I says, I'd be dead in
ten minutes.

Him and the sergeant had another conference over
in the corner, a little louder this time. I could hear most
of it. I heard the sergeant suggesting what I had already
thought of, that they just shoot me and forge my name.
But the captain said they had to handle this so that dog

of a magistrate would accept it. The magistrate was a man with a gavel where his heart should be. He had no woman, and he slept with his lawbooks instead. He was a stickler for observing the last fine point of the law and was rich enough that he did not need to take the *mordida*. Worse, he was kin of the governor, so they didn't dare force him. Worst of all, he knowed my face and he knowed my signature. I had signed it in front of him when I bought the ranch.

The captain never would of made a poker player. I could read his face when he came back. He had decided to give me what I asked for. They probably figured they could still kill me at the river and get the gold back after I had signed the paper. But he had to try one more time.

He says, "*Gringo*, you ask for too much."

"It ain't much of a ride from here to the river," says I. "You want the ranch, and I want a sporting chance to live."

He gave in finally, like I knowed he would, though it killed his soul to bend so much for a lousy *gringo*. He sent the sergeant out, and in a little while he was back and said everything was ready. They had a detail of half a dozen men waiting outside of the office on horseback. They had throwed my saddle on a sorry plug that couldn't of outrun the rest of them if they had all had one leg broke.

I told the captain there was one more thing I wanted, my watch with Millie's picture in it. The sergeant had it, and it tore him plumb up to give it to me. He opened the case and let it play its little tune before he would turn it over. I reckon he was afraid it would get shot to pieces when they finished me off.

I didn't know exactly what I was going to do when I got to the river. I figured the only real chance I had was to make a wild sashay and jump into the water before they could stop me. Naturally they would shoot at me every time I came up for air, but I would just have to try not to breathe much. I had already seen that they wasn't very good shots.

It bothered me about the gold. I couldn't swim across with that big sack; it would take me under. But maybe that little bag wouldn't hurt. I says to the captain, "Been thinking I'd sure like to carry the gold."

He looks at me like I'm crazy and says, "You have not signed yet. You get the money when you sign."

"The little bag at least," I says. "Just let me enjoy the feel of it."

He handed it to me. Maybe he felt like it would keep my greed fired up and I wouldn't give him no more trouble about the deed. I kept feeling the gold, which I knowed was what he wanted me to do. The seat of my britches was all itchy from wanting to get this over with, from wanting to get away from them. But I did enjoy the smell of the good clean air. It was the first time I'd been out in the open in three days.

The captain made it a point for us to ride by the government house and to call out the magistrate so he could see me with his own eyes. He told him we was all on our way down to the office of the lawyer to sign some papers. I spoke up to invite the magistrate to go along with us, but the sergeant stuck a pistol in my back where the magistrate couldn't see it, and I had to give up on hospitality.

There wasn't no bridges over the river in them days, nowhere on the whole Rio Grande. There wasn't even a ferry at this point. There was just a place about fifty yards wide that you could swim a horse across. Wagons and carts and such had to go down the river a long ways to where there was a little cable-operated ferry.

Texas looked pretty good to me, laying over yonder across that little stream of muddy water. Sure, the law was hunting for me over there, or at least I thought they was. But looking across, I couldn't see a sign of anybody on the other side. I didn't hardly expect that there would be somebody come over and help me out of the predicament I was in.

The captain was getting awful impatient. He turns to me and says, "Here we are, just the way we promised you. Now, the deed . . ."

I had kept edging to the front, getting as near to the river as I could for my big break. But that sergeant outguessed me. He rode in close and taken the reins of that sorry plug I was on. If I ran for the river now I was going to have to do it afoot. I sort of measured the sergeant with my eye, figuring how to climb right over him.

I says to the captain, "Do I have your word that when I sign, I can cross the river and you won't shoot me in the back?"

You ever see a rattlesnake curl his lips back? That's the kind of smile the captain gave me. "You have my word. The word of an officer and a gentleman."

He was lying like a candidate. The soldiers began to back their horses away and form up a line. I knowed what was coming to me the minute I signed that paper. I had got to the river all right, but I was never going to cross it.

One word you never want to say is *never*. All of a sudden the whole thing was taken out of his hands.

There come, in the wink of an eye, a volley of guns like the Fourth of July. For a sorry old plug like he was, that horse of mine must of jumped four feet straight up. The sergeant fell off with his face all bloody and hit the sand and just laid there. His horse taken out in a panic and swam across the river. I finally got my spooked plug under control and looked around and seen half of them soldiers down just like the sergeant was. The rest of them was running off, all but the captain. He just sat there looking sort of foolish and drained out.

Down to the riverbank came a dozen or so ragged-looking Mexicans with guns smoking in their hands. I didn't know the faces, but I sure knowed the type. They was a bunch of them cattle-stealing rebels. Directly I seen a friendly face coming. At least, I thought it was friendly. Felipe Rios rode down to where me and the captain was. With him was that rebel leader that I'd had such a cuss fight with over them running my cattle off.

I was never more glad to see a Mexican in my life, hardly. I says, "Felipe, you sure have a way of turning up when a man needs you."

The captain just looked at them and swallowed. He still held the deed in his hand. I noticed that the hand was trembling a right smart. He says, "I was about to release this man." Which was true; he was about to release me from all worldly cares. Felipe reached up and jerked the deed away from him, looked at it and handed it to the leader. I remembered then that Felipe couldn't read. But that rebel could.

Now that I seen the two of them together, the resemblance was considerable. I would of bet they was first cousins, at least.

That rebel studied the paper and knowed in a minute what this whole thing was about. Says he, "*Gringo*, we thought they were simply going to take you out and kill you. But it appears there was more."

I ought to've knowed not to talk so much, but I was so glad to see them that I had no caution. I told them what Santos had figured on doing, and what I was planning to try to do.

He didn't look a bit pleased. He says, "You would have turned your property over to this butcher to save your own neck?"

I told him it was the only neck I had, and the property wouldn't of helped me much if I was dead.

He looked at the canvas sack on the captain's saddle. "You were going to sell it to him for money. That is like a *gringo*."

Where I came from it was always customary to sell

things for money. It was the best medium of exchange anybody had ever come up with. But I got a strong feeling that I wasn't in no position to argue details. I wasn't in no position to argue *anything*. The look in his eyes told me I'd better do a lot of listening.

He filled my ear with a lot of stuff about how they was fighting to stop oppression and bury the butchers like Santos and so forth, and about how hard it was for them to understand a *gringo* whose only interest was in money when there was people bleeding and dying all around.

The only ones I could see bleeding and dying right then was Santos's soldiers. They was in a bad way, the ones that hadn't gotten clear. I wouldn't of given a well-used chaw of tobacco for Santos's chances of leaving that riverbank alive, either. I think the only question they had about him was whether to slit his throat from the left or from the right. And he knowed it, too, because his face was drained from a nice brown down to about a *gringo* color.

The rebel shoved the deed back at me and says, "You were going to sign it for him. Sign it for me!"

I looked at Felipe. He wasn't going to be no help this time, I could tell. All his sympathy was with them others. We had come to the parting of the ways. I reached up and taken a lead pencil out of Santos's pocket, one he had brought for that purpose, only things hadn't turned in quite the direction he had intended. I signed the deed and handed it to the rebel. I asks, "Who gets the ranch?"

Felipe says, "María."

I couldn't argue much with that. It seemed proper, since she had been a partner in it anyway.

I says, "And who gets María?"

Felipe says, "I do."

I figured he already had, maybe even while Jackson was still there. Well, that meant he would get the ranch too, which was better than having it go to Santos. Or to that rebel leader, who didn't look much like a cow-boy to me noway. He had that wild eye you see in people who are always going around over creation looking for something to raise hell about.

I reached to get the canvas bag of gold off of San-tos's saddle. "That belongs to me," I says.

The rebel clamped his hand over mine. He says, "No! You have just given it to our cause. We have use for it."

He started telling me again about their great crusade, and about all the hungry and shirtless and barefoot ones, and I knowed damn well there wouldn't none of them ever see any of this money. It's always been my observation that the feller who hollers loudest about helping the downtrodden poor is usually counting him-self at the head of the list. Soon as he gets his hands on some money of his own, the poor don't look near as hungry to him anymore.

I told him it didn't hardly seem right to leave me without a thing to show for all my trouble. I was giving up my ranch; I ought to have *something*.

They didn't know about that little bag of gold in my shirt.

"You have your life, *gringo*," he says. "It is not worth much, but it is more than Santos was going to give you. Now go, before we take that too!"

Everybody's eyes was on me right at that minute. Santos taken what little chance he had. He jabbed his spurs into that horse and jumped him off into the water as hard as he could run, taking gold and all. He caught them rebels by surprise. When they finally started shooting at him, he slid out of the saddle to make less of a target. Somewhere out there he got separated from the horse and had to try to swim by himself. I don't know if a bullet caught him, or if his clothes pulled him down, or if he just plain couldn't swim. In a min-ute or two there wasn't no sign of him anyplace. He was gone, under that muddy water. Next time he ever came up, he was going to be a long ways down the river, and deader than yesterday's fish.

His horse must of been boogered by the shooting. It went right on swimming across toward the Texas side.

I had shaken hands with Felipe and said good-bye to my ranch, so I started swimming that plug of mine across too. I kind of halfway expected them rebels to decide to send me along after Santos, but they didn't. I got to the Texas bank without any holes in me that wasn't natural.

I had it in my head that luck was with me, and that I'd wind up with that canvas bag of gold and silver after all. I caught up to Santos's horse where it had stopped to rest itself on the Texas side. The sergeant's horse was standing there with it.

The bag was gone. It had slipped loose somewhere out there in the river.

Santos might float to the top, eventually, but that bag never would.

At least I still had the little sack of gold I had hidden in my shirt. And I had three horses, if the plug I was riding was to be counted as a horse. The captain's was a well-built black with an American brand. He had a pretty good Mexican-style saddle on him, and a carbine in a scabbard, so that I wasn't plumb unarmed. There was a saber on the saddle. I started to throw it away, till I decided maybe I could trade it later for supplies. Waste not, want not.

The shooting was liable to draw somebody curious. I didn't want to be there to explain things to them when they showed up, so I got on the captain's black horse and led the other two and taken out for the thickest brush I could see.

I was glad to be in Texas again. Hell, I was glad to be *alive*.

Chapter 3

Of course I was still Joe Peeler then, and you the world know me now as Joe Pepper. You want to know how come me to get to be Joe Pepper? Well, I'll tell you if you'll be patient.

For a while there I was in an awful uncomfortable situation. There wasn't but two sides to the river, and I was in some demand on both of them. The best bet I had was to go west as far and as fast as I could without doing me or the horses any real hurt.

The Texas and Mexico border had a lot of variety in them days, same as it does now. Down on the very lowest part, toward Brownsville, there was getting to be a certain amount of farming on both sides of the river, and the country was settling up. It was a good fertile land where cold weather didn't bite very hard or very long, and just about anything you wanted to plant would grow. Go up the river a hundred or so miles, though, and you start to get into a desert type of country where a man trying to farm had better have himself some awful big buckets to carry water out to his crops. You'd find that the farmers, especially over on the Mexico side, would dig irrigation ditches to carry water to fields about three times the size of a postage stamp. Back away from the river it was mostly just ranchland. Good ranchland, everything considered, only you had to give your cattle lots of room and not let them see too much of each other or they would soon be overstocked.

It was a big old wide-open country where you could go for a long time and never run across a lawman, or where you might—if your luck ran sour—turn a corner in a wagon road and run into a whole covey of Texas Rangers.

There was a good many people in that section them days that wasn't very popular where they had come from and couldn't go back home without some risk of winding up as guests of the state. But down in the border country they might go for years—maybe forever—and not have to answer any embarrassing questions. As long as they didn't raise any undue hell, people didn't worry overly much about where they had come from or what the homefolks might of thought about them.

If I had been in trouble in some other state, or even up in East Texas, I might of stayed in that lower border country and never had to worry about old times. But I had shot Jesse Ordway in South Texas, not far from the Rio Grande. I felt like the risk was too much for me to put up with. Sooner or later, the way people had of drifting west, I'd come face to face with somebody who knowed who I was and knowed about Jesse Ordway. It stood to reason that Mrs. Ordway had posted a reward on me. She was rich enough to've made it a big one.

A lot of people are good about minding their own business as long as it don't cost them nothing, but you put money into the situation and they come down with a bad case of public responsibility.

I had three horses on my hands, and a saddle for each of them. A man leading two saddled horses just naturally attracts attention. People get to wondering who used to fill the saddles, and they think maybe he knows something he ain't telling. A few miles from where I had crossed the river I came upon a young Mexican boy herding a bunch of spotted goats on a paint pony, bareback. I gave him the sergeant's saddle. He was a little dubious about it till I told him it had come to me in a vision that I was supposed to give it to the first boy I came across herding goats on a paint pony. He was a religious boy, evidently, because he taken it.

I was kind of tempted to keep the captain's saddle because it was made of good leather and had some fancy silver on it. But a man that ain't used to them big-horned Mexico saddles generally has trouble with them at first. They'll pinch right where it grabs you the worst. I came onto a Mexican packtrain loaded down with contraband Mexican liquor heading north to San Antonio. I traded that saddle to them smugglers for a sackful of *tamales* that they had packed in lard to eat along the way, and a goatskin full of raw *pulque*. I tell you, a man that drinks a little old-time *pulque* every day ought not to ever have to worry about a tapeworm. There ain't nothing could live bottled up amidst that stuff. It taken a right smart of it to burn the stench of that cell out of my nose. There I was with a little leather pouch full of gold coins, and all them tamales and that *pulque*, plus two good horses and one plug. I was rich, when you figure the times.

But a man can get tired of *tamales* pretty quick when they're all he has to eat. It was mostly Mexicans living along the border then, whichever side of it you happened to be on. One evening I reined in to a place and found a young Mexican woman there all by herself

without so much as a pony to ride if she had to go
anyplace. She said she was married, and her husband
was off someplace on business. By the conversation I
got a pretty good notion what kind of business it was;
there was people on the Texas side that used to raid
the ranches there and sell stolen cattle and horses and
mules down in Mexico, and people on the Mexican
side would drive up stolen stock from Mexico to sell
in Texas. Sometimes the same horse might change
ownership three-four times and wind up back where he
started from. It made for a lot of business, anyway.
Like I was saying, the woman had been by herself a
good spell, and I found her mighty lonesome, same as
I was. She never said it in so many words, but I figured
she had already made up her mind that her husband
was dead. Oftentimes when them outlaws got shot,
whichever side of the river it was on, the people who
killed them just left them laying where they was, and
nobody ever heard from them again. It wasn't no easy
life.

I stayed there with that woman three, maybe four
days, resting up the horses, filling up on her cooking,
comforting her in her loneliness. When I left there I
just taken two of the horses with me. I left her that
plug.

Past Laredo, and especially beyond Eagle Pass,
things got pretty thin on the border. It started to getting
into Indian country, and things tended sometimes to be
a little wild for a man of genteel tastes. The government had a military post on upriver that they called
Fort Clark, and the troops there was kept busy most of
the time running after Indians and renegades that had
learned how to use the border to their advantage. There
was Lipan Apaches and Kickapoos and the like down
there, all of them kind of having it in for the *gringo*.
Folks told me the Kickapoos had been friendly Indians
one time, never gave nobody any trouble till a bunch
of Confederate soldiers—this was during the war, you

know—mistaken them for a bunch of hostiles and plowed into them on one of the creeks that run into the Concho. It came as a surprise to the Indians, first, then a big surprise to the soldiers because them Indians turned around and whipped the britches off of them. After that, they was enemy Indians like all the others.

I'd never fought no Indians up to that time, and hadn't lost any, but I figured it would be about as unhealthy for me to run into a bunch of soldiers as a bunch of Indians, so I tried to skirt around all the posts and towns and such. I was on one of them wide sashays when I got the name of Joe Pepper.

I hadn't seen any Indian sign that I could recognize. Up to this time I'd never even seen or been around Indians anyhow, except them few on the cattle trail to Kansas, and they wasn't really wild. Maybe I didn't know what to look for. But to play it safe I would stop early of an evening and build me a little campfire while it was still light, cook me some supper, kill the fire and move on a ways till it got dark, then make a cold camp. I didn't want Indians finding me at night by seeing my campfire or by smelling the smoke from it.

So one evening a while before sundown I was cooking up some *tortillas* out of ground corn I'd got from the woman, and boiling coffee in a can, when I seen a feller come riding in from the east. I could tell right off that he wasn't no Indian, and I had a feeling by the looks of him that he wasn't a lawman. You get a sixth sense about lawmen if you spend long enough avoiding them. So I hailed him to come on in and invited him to share what vittles I had. He was a tallish sort of a gent, with stubbly whiskers—rusty-colored—that hadn't felt a razor in quite a spell. I could tell by the way he wolfed down them *tamales*—cold lard and all— that he hadn't eaten a good square meal in a while. You never seen a man more needful than he was, or so grateful for what he was given. It kind of gave me a glow inside to know how much good I was doing for a needy and grateful stranger.

Now, if you've ever heard anybody cock a hammer back on a pistol, and that pistol is pointed at you, it's a sound you'll never forget the rest of your life. It's like a rattle-snake's rattle—you can hear it a hundred yards away. I whirled around and tried to grab my rifle. But I was too late.

That grateful stranger shot me.

I can't swear that I heard it. I seen a flash, but I can't even swear it was from the gun. It might of been from the pain when that thing hit me in the ribs. I remember feeling like I'd been kicked by a Missouri mule—a big one at that—and I went down like I had been sledged. I remember fighting for breath and not getting any. I remember that grateful stranger feeling around over me, finding that little bag of gold in my shirt and stripping me to the waist to see if I had any more money. And I remember the warm feel of the blood running down my hide.

It's bad enough having somebody shoot you. It's that much worse when he makes you feel like six kinds of a fool for letting him. I remember laying there trying to get a breath so I could cuss him, and cuss myself for letting him into my camp.

Better it had been the Indians. They wasn't in the habit of repaying a kindness by killing you. Of course, there wasn't many people them days bent over backwards to be kind to Indians.

For a long time I figured I was dead, and I wondered how it was that I could be laying there thinking about it. I couldn't move . . . couldn't even breathe, hardly. I couldn't see enough to tell, but I was satisfied he had run off with everything I had.

It was getting on dark when somebody came along and found me. Things was so hazy by then that I couldn't tell much. I knowed they lifted me up onto a big wagon or something, and I could tell it hurt like thunder. They probed around my gizzard with a knife. By this time, of course, I knowed I wasn't dead—yet. I figured they would kill me off, though, the way they was doing. The pain got so bad that I passed out. Next thing I remembered, I was riding on my back in something that felt like a wagon, and every time it hit a bump it was like somebody had jabbed me in the ribs with a crowbar. It was an awful bumpy road.

I got clear enough in my head to know they was talking Mexican, not *gringo*. It didn't make much difference at the time. Way after dark they stopped and lifted me down. They laid me on a blanket and gave me a big drink of some kind of liquor and covered me up.

Come daylight I could see that I was amongst some Mexican freighters. They had a bunch of oxen and them old big high-wheeled carts that you still see now and again down in the border country. They asked me if I felt like having any breakfast. I didn't, but I wanted another drink. Turned out it was *tequila*. You probably wouldn't know about this, preacher, but *tequila* ain't half bad when you're in need of it.

I gradually sat up and began to take stock. My ribs was sore as the devil, but I wasn't near as bad off as I had a right to be, getting shot in the side that way. I asked them what they had done to me. They said they had dug out a bullet that was laying in beneath the skin, up against the ribs. One of the Mexicans—a boy of fifteen or sixteen, I'd judge—brought it to show to me. It was flattened out, like if you'd laid it on a rail and let a train run over it the way kids will do sometimes with a coin, when they don't know the value of money. I knowed old Joe Peeler was tough, but I didn't see how I could of taken a slug and flattened it out that much and lived to look at it.

Then I realized that grateful stranger had shot me in the gold pouch. I had that leather bag under my shirt, and as I wheeled around his bullet had caught it. The gold coins taken up most of the force so that it was nearly spent by the time it got through to me. I had bled like a stuck hog, though. He must of figured I was near dead or he'd of seen to it.

Every move I made brought a little jab that made me use the Lord's name in vain. I always figured that was one of the lesser Commandments, and since I had already broke so many of the bigger ones, I didn't see what harm could come of it. It helps a man feel better sometimes to cuss a little, like you'd stick a knife into a bloated steer to let the gas out and relieve the pressure on him.

Them Mexicans was good to me. I felt bad that I didn't have a thing I could pay them with. The stranger had taken the gold, my horses, my rifle, my *tamales*, my *pulque* . . . everything but my boots. My feet must not of been his size.

I've always had a kindly feeling toward Mexicans since that time. Them freighters was God's people because they could just as well of left me laying where they found me. They sure didn't owe me nothing, a *gringo* stranger like I was, and trouble to boot. They wasn't of your church, preacher; maybe they didn't go to no church. But they was God's people.

I laid on top of the load on one of them big carts and rode all day. Along toward night we come to a settlement named Catclaw. It had some older Mexican name, but the *gringos* had come along and changed it. It was still Mexican, mostly. But I could tell by the names on the stores that it had a share of *gringos* in it. It was a county seat, too, because it had a frame courthouse up on the town square. It takes a *gringo* to want to build something frame when the lumber's got to be hauled three hundred miles, and when they've got all the material within a mile that they need to build out of adobe or rock. Next to the courthouse, almost as big and a lot stronger built, was a rock jail with walls that must of been a foot and a half thick. Looking at it even from a distance, I could almost smell that Mexican cell again. It always made me a little sick to my stomach if I thought about it much. You never know what freedom is really worth till you've done without.

I hadn't made any plans. I was broke, afoot, and for all I knowed had a price on my head. I had it in my mind that I would wait till way up in the night, then steal me a horse and cross back over the river into Mexico again. I was far enough west that I doubted my troubles from downriver would find me.

It never occurred to me that them freighters would take matters out of my hands. I was sitting around the fire with them at supper, eating a bite and trying to figure out exactly what I was going to do, when somebody came up from behind me. I thought it was one of the freighters till he spoke out in *gringo*. He says, "I understand you've had some trouble."

I turned around right quick, and there stood a man with a badge on his shirt. That badge looked as big as the lid on a five-gallon bucket. I let my hand drop down to my belt where my six-shooter would of been, if I'd had one. I figured he had me.

I says, "No, I ain't had no trouble to speak of."

The sheriff says, "They tell me somebody shot you and robbed you and left you to die. If that ain't trouble, I'd hate to see what trouble is." He acted kind of out of patience.

I told him I had no earthly idea who the grateful stranger was, or where he had gone to, so there wasn't much either me or the law could do. I thanked him kindly and told him I was sorry he had bothered himself.

By then he was getting suspicious, because most people in my shape would of been hollering for the law to drop everything else and help them. He says, "What's your name, friend?"

Him being a sheriff and all, I sure didn't figure he had much cause to be calling me friend. And I sure wasn't going to tell him my name was Joe Peeler. I looked across the fire and saw one of the Mexicans pop a hot *chiltipiquin* pepper into his mouth. Right quick I said my name was Pepper . . . Joe Pepper.

If I'd said my name was Smith, like so many of them do, he'd of knowed I was lying. But I suppose Pepper sounded natural enough, because he taken it for the gospel truth. He says, "Well, Joe Pepper, how would you like to come down to the office with me?"

I can tell you, I didn't like the idea atall. I figured he had a nice little cell waiting for me, and there wasn't a blessed thing I could do to protect myself. I says, "Any particular reason?" Seemed like a foolish question at the time.

He says, "I've got a stack of flyers over there with descriptions of various and sundry fugitives. Maybe you'll find your man on one of them. It would help, at least, if we know who we're hunting for."

I could think of twenty-seven places I had rather of gone than to a sheriff's office, but he had a gun in his belt, and that gave him a right smart advantage.

I figured at the time that he knowed who I really was and intended to slam the door shut on me soon as he got me inside. But he didn't. His office was a little box of a room in the front end of the jail. He motioned for me to sit down. He went to rifling through a drawer of a big roll-top desk and brought out a stack of papers. He says, "I'm taking it for granted you can read."

Lots of people couldn't, you know. But I told him sure, I'd been reading since I was ten-eleven years old. Slow about it, sometimes, but I could read. He handed me the papers and told me to go through them. While I was reading he would go rustle us some coffee.

By then I decided he didn't suspicion who I was. And all of a sudden I figured it would be an advantage for me to go through the flyers. I could find the one on me, stick it in my pocket when he wasn't looking, and he would never miss it. Soon as he left the room I went through the papers right fast, looking for one on me. When I got to the last one in the stack, I hadn't found anything. I went back through them again, a little slower. But it wasn't there.

At that time I still had no idea that Mrs. Ordway never had pressed any charges against me. I figured maybe the mail was slow; it wasn't fast and efficient like it is now. They even lost stuff, sometimes. Well, I thought, if I could stay out ahead of the reward notices, maybe I would be all right till I got out of Texas. New Mexico and Arizona was big places, and California was even bigger. A man could lose himself.

I went back through the notices a third time, taking it slow and reading each one. When I got through, I had pulled out three that sort of fit the grateful stranger. The sheriff came in with a pot of coffee he had made or had had made for him someplace else. He looked at the three and wadded up one of them. "I ought to've pulled this one," he says. "I got word he was killed in Laredo. Killed by a wagon. A hundred law officers after him and he got run over by a beer wagon." He studied the other two. Especially one of them.

"Owen Rainwater," he says. "He could sure be the one; he's ornery enough. He's got a brother that lives up north of here. Owen's bad. Harvey's a lot worse."

I figured that wherever I could find Harvey Rainwater, I could probably find Owen Rainwater too. And my horses. And maybe my gold, if he hadn't already spent it. I says, "How do I get to Harvey Rainwater's?"

"You ain't going," he says. "Whatever he stole, it ain't worth the trip."

I told him I had already made a fair trip; a little extra wouldn't hurt me. But he says, "It'd be the longest short trip you ever made. If you need money, Pepper, I can probably find you enough work around here to get you a little road stake. You don't want to be messing around with them Rainwaters."

I told him I didn't intend to mess around with them;

I just intended to get back what belonged to me. He told me to forget about it; I was probably still running a fever from that wound and I would get over it in a few days.

The Mexican freighters moved on next morning, soon as it was daylight. I thanked them all very kindly for what they had done for me, and they wished me all the best of luck and went with them big carts. You could hear the wooden wheels squeaking for a mile.

The sheriff had it fixed up for me to sleep in a wagonyard and help fork hay to the horses and such in return for three meals a day till I was feeling better and could either move on or get me a better job. It wasn't much, but I decided to stick with it a few days till my side quit hurting and I felt like I could handle a long ride. I was still figuring on borrowing me a good horse some dark night.

I didn't have to go. The second day, I was raking spilled hay up off of the ground and putting it back into a wooden rack when my eye was caught by a man riding one horse and leading another down the street. At the distance I couldn't tell much about him except that he was tall. But I knowed the horses; they was the Santos black and the bay I had inherited from the late sergeant.

I dropped the rake and went into the barn. I had already noticed that the feller who owned the wagonyard kept a big rifle in there on a rack. It was some kind of handmade rifle, manufactured for the Confederacy by a homegrown armory over in East Texas. He just stared at me when I taken that rifle down and asked him for the loan of two-three cartridges. Naturally he wanted to know what I was going to do with the gun, and I told him I thought I had seen a coyote.

He went on to tell me the rifle wasn't none too accurate at long range . . . it was one of them hurry-up war jobs. I told him I figured I'd stalk this coyote and get up close. He gave me half a dozen cartridges. I figured I wouldn't use more than one, if I used any atall; I never was wasteful with high-priced ammunition.

The two horses was tied in front of an adobe saloon, which was to be expected. I would've found it funny if that grateful stranger had tied them at the church. The stable man followed me out and watched me start down the street. I don't suppose he had ever seen a coyote shot in town.

I stopped and looked at the horses. They wasn't any the worse for wear as far as I could tell. They looked the same as when I had lost them. The black had my saddle on him. I didn't see no sense in waiting; that stranger was in the saloon spending my money. I cocked the hammer back and stepped through the door.

I don't suppose you ever watched a man look at a ghost. That was my rusty-bearded friend, all right; I knowed it the second I laid eyes on him. He sat there staring at me like he couldn't believe what he seen. He dropped a glass that was half full of whiskey and let it spill all over the little square table he was sitting at. There was another man sitting with him. He couldn't figure out what the trouble was.

I says to the stranger, "You borrowed some things that belong to me. I come to get them back."

Along about then he decided I wasn't no ghost, and I wasn't dead. He didn't have anything to say for himself. He just reached down for the pistol at his hip.

That "wanted" notice in the sheriff's office had said something about Owen Rainwater being dangerous with a gun, and I suppose he was when he stood behind a man, like he had done with me. But face to face he just wasn't much. He never did get his pistol clean out of the holster.

One thing about it, when you shot a man with one of them big old rifles close up, they didn't have to hold an autopsy over him to find out if he was dead. He just laid there on his back on the dirt floor with one leg all tangled up in his chair.

I always figured the reason people like Owen Rainwater shot men in the back was because they knowed their limitations.

That friend of his at the table with him was considerable agitated. I reloaded the rifle real fast in case I might have to reason with him. But he wasn't much on this face-to-face business. He ran mostly to talk.

He hollers, "You know what you done? You killed Owen Rainwater!"

I says, "That was sure my intention."

He goes on hollering about what a big man Owen Rainwater was, and what a big man his brother Harvey was, and how bad Harvey was going to feel about this. I told him I was sorry if I had caused anybody any undue inconvenience; I had just come to get back what was mine.

I felt of Rainwater's pockets, and sure enough he had my sack of gold. I had to take it out kind of careful to keep from spilling coins. The sack had a big hole in it. It also had a dark stain that I knowed was from my blood. It didn't make me feel atall sorry for what I had done. I held the sack up for the bartender and a couple of the customers to see.

Says I, "I'm just taking back what's mine. He stole this from me."

They didn't seem disposed to argue about it. They was as agreeable a bunch as you could ask for. That friend of Rainwater's, he seemed to decide he wasn't thirsty anymore, because when I looked around he was gone. I taken Rainwater's pistols . . . figured they was fitting interest for the use of my horses and gold.

You've probably noticed how a gunshot or two tends to draw a crowd. In two or three minutes that little saloon was jammed so full of people that it was hard to draw a breath. There wasn't anything left in there that I was interested in. I went out front to see after my horses. Pretty soon the sheriff came trotting up, puffing pretty good. He was carrying some extra weight for what frame he had. He says, "What's going on in there?"

I told him nothing was going on in there now; it was all over with. I told him I had just got my property back. Seemed like he pretty well pictured the rest of it, because he said for me to stay right where I was at, and he went inside. In a minute he was back outside with me, awful flustered.

He says, "Do you know you just killed Owen Rainwater?"

I told him I'd already had that pointed out to me. I told him I was reclaiming my horses and hoped I wasn't going to have to argue with anybody over it, because I was getting awful tired. He said if they was my horses I was welcome to take them.

Then he said something that I ought to have remembered for myself but had somehow forgot. It was a thing that kind of set the pattern of Joe Pepper's life for a long time afterwards.

He says, "You know, there's a reward for Owen Rainwater."

He had gotten me interested. I says, "How much?"

He scratched his head and wrinkled up his face like it hurt him to think so hard. He says, "About five hundred dollars, best I recall. Maybe it was a little more. I'd have to go look at the flyer." Then he twisted up his face even worse. "But it'd take several days to get it cleared and paid to you. You'll need to be moving on. That's too bad, because I'll bet you could of used that money."

You know how it feels to have somebody wave money at you and then take it away? Sort of grates at you, it does. I says, "I ain't in no hurry."

"You ought to be," he tells me. "When Harvey Rainwater finds out about this he'll come looking for you. He ain't no man you'll want to fool with."

"I wasn't fooling with his brother Owen," says I. "Is there a reward on Harvey too?"

The sheriff's jaw dropped down to about the second button. "You don't think you're going to take him *too*?"

"Well, sir," says I, "as long as I got to wait around anyway, I'd just as well turn my hand to a little paying labor."

He stared at me like he couldn't figure out what breed of horse I was. Finally he says, "You know what I ought to do? I ought to deputize you so whatever you do'll be legal."

I would of had to study on that some; the idea of me carrying a badge didn't set real good with me right then. But in a minute he taken it all back anyhow. He says, "I can't afford to do that. Harvey'd kill you, and then he'd be mad at me because I had pinned a badge on you. I don't think I favor getting him mad at me."

I says, "If he's such a wanted man, why ain't you been out there hunting for him yourself?"

"Three reasons," says Sheriff Smathers. "First place, he's in another county. Second place, he's never caused us no trouble here, up to now. Third place, he'd shoot hell out of me."

I questioned the sheriff pretty sharp on whether he really thought Rainwater would be coming into town looking for me. He said he would bet his life on it. Seemed more like he was betting *my* life. I could think of lots of things I'd rather do than sit around there waiting for somebody to come in and kill me on his own terms.

One reason I had gotten Owen so easy was that I had taken him by surprise. That gave me a little advantage. I figured maybe the smart thing to do was surprise Harvey Rainwater, too.

I asked the sheriff where to find him. For a lawman talking about an outlaw he was supposed to go out and get for himself, he sure seemed to know a lot of details.

He told me about every wagon track, every cowtrail and rat's nest between town and the adobe *rancho* where Rainwater was holed up.

I asked him how I would know Harvey when I seen him. He says, "Just remember what his brother looked like. Add ten or fifteen pounds of flesh and thirty pounds of meanness. That'll be Harvey."

I bought me a few traveling supplies and some fresh cartridges. I told the sheriff to get things moving on the rewards for both of the Rainwater boys, because I would be back to collect.

He seemed to doubt me.

The way I figured it—and the sheriff had agreed with me—the friend who had been in the saloon sipping whiskey with Owen had probably lit a shuck to tell Harvey. Brotherly love being what it was— it always seemed to me that the worst of kinfolks stuck together better than respectable kinfolks—Harvey Rainwater would probably not waste no time heading for town to hunt for me. He would figure it was a cinch I'd leave, so he would move at a good clip. From the sheriff's description it was going to take that friend till way up in the night to get to Harvey. More than likely Harvey would start for town as soon as it was daylight.

I rode till a while before dark, then stopped and fixed me a bite of supper over a small fire that wouldn't put out much smoke. Folks said there wasn't much to worry about from Indians in that part of the country, but there was worse things than Indians. I put the fire out and rode a ways more into the dark, like had become my habit. I knowed where I was going. The sheriff said the wagon trail led up to within a few miles of where Harvey was staying. All I had to do was keep on the trail.

I had me a good night's sleep with that gold sack in my shirt. Odd, how much comfort a man gets out of a handful of coin, especially when it's got that yellow color. I've had pretty women sing good night to me, and their songs wasn't half as sweet as the clinking of them gold coins, one against another.

Next morning I had me some coffee and bacon and started up the trail. Outside of cattle, I didn't see much till upwards of dinnertime. Then I seen half a dozen horseback riders way off in the distance. I watched them till I decided they was sure-enough coming my way. I knowed within reason who they'd be—one of them, anyhow. I slipped Santos's carbine out of the scabbard and pulled off into some brush and settled myself down to wait.

You'll find lots of people who like pistols, and I always carried one, but if you want something to really display your authority, show them the front end of a rifle or a carbine. That'll get their attention every time. I just sat there amidst the greenery of the mesquite and catclaw and let them ride on past me. They didn't see me, of course, because people don't generally see me when I don't want them to. I didn't have no trouble recognizing Harvey Rainwater. He was Owen Rainwater all over again, and about two collar sizes bigger around the neck. He had a look on his face like some of them old vigilantes must of had a long time ago when they was getting ready to break in a new rope.

I pulled my horse out into the trail, stepped down behind him so I didn't show too much of myself, and I hollers, "Harvey Rainwater!"

My voice always carried good. He turned his horse around real quick. I don't know which he seen first, me or my carbine. He didn't know me, of course, but a shooting iron has a way of introducing itself.

He couldn't see me very well, which is the way I wanted it. I never was one to take undue advantage, just enough so I'd be sure to win. He says, "Who are you?"

Says I, "My name is Joe Pepper. I believe you're hunting for me. I come out to save you a long trip."

The tall feller was riding alongside him, the one who

had been with Owen Rainwater in the saloon. He recognized me right off. I heard him say, "That's him, Harvey. That's the gink that done it."

I says, "Owen taken what was mine, and I taken it back. He shot me once when I wasn't looking. He was looking straight at me when I shot *him*. Now, I ain't asking for trouble with you, Harvey, but if you want me I'm at your convenience."

He just looked at me like he couldn't believe none of it. A lot of them old boys earned a reputation for being quick on the trigger and dangerous, but most often that was only when they had everything going for them the way they planned it. Catch them on their left foot and they're uncertain which way to turn.

I says, "You other boys, if you ain't relatives of his, I'd advise you to stay out. I don't like hurting a man when it ain't necessary."

He said something to the men that was with him, and they all pulled off to one side except the tall one. Harvey reached for his pistol. I let him get a grip on it and start bringing it up before I squeezed the trigger. I didn't want it said afterwards that I killed a man whose gun was still in the holster. That bullet taken him about six inches under his chin. His pistol went off and grazed his horse's right forefoot. That horse broke to pitching and sent him sailing out there like a big old floppy bird.

I doubt as Harvey Rainwater ever knowed it.

My own horse was cutting up, too. He didn't like the way I had used the seat of my saddle for a gunrest. I levered another cartridge into the chamber and brought it back up to my shoulder because I didn't know what the rest of Rainwater's crew was apt to do. All of them just sat there looking dumb except the tall one. He drawed a gun and was bringing it down on me when I let him have what was in the carbine. It sure seemed to come as a surprise to him. His horse made a couple of jumps, and the tall man wound up laying on top of Harvey Rainwater.

I watched the other four real close, afraid one of them might take a notion to do something rash. But they was all well-behaved.

I says to them, "I've had about enough of this. Any more kinfolks amongst you?"

They was quick to let me know they wasn't kin, just friends. And friendship has its limits. One of them pointed to the tall man. "Slim yonder, he was the only one that was kin. He was a cousin to Harvey and Owen. They wasn't too bright on his side of the family."

I didn't say so, but it seemed to me like the whole Rainwater tribe had been shorted some on brains. I says, "Well, if you boys are sure you ain't got no further quarrel with me, I'd be much obliged if you'd all drop your guns right where you're at." They seemed agreeable to that. It didn't take but a minute. I says, "Nobody's going to disturb them guns. You-all can come back here in an hour or two and get them. But right now I'd like to see how far you can get in the shortest possible time, right back the direction you came from."

They done pretty good, I thought.

When they was a fair distance and still going, I commenced catching up the Rainwater horses and petting them and talking to them gentle to calm them down. You can talk to a horse a right smart easier than you can talk to some people. They was a little skittish about me putting the Rainwaters back up onto them. They was used to a man riding head up instead of head down. My side was still hurting me a little, too, from where Owen Rainwater's bullet had hit me in the ribs. But directly I got the two tied into place. I looked back once to be sure where the other four was at and found they had understood me real well. They was still riding off.

*　　*　　*

I've always had a suspicion that Sheriff Smathers turned in for the reward on Owen Rainwater and figured to keep it himself. The last thing he expected was to see me come riding back down that street with two more Rainwaters tied across their saddles. I pulled up in front of his office at the jail and hollered for him to come out. He just stood there leaning against the doorjamb like he thought he might fall, otherwise. He finally came down the steps and walked around and pulled up the two Rainwaters' heads to take a good look at the faces.

He kept saying over and over again, "I'll be damned! I'll be damned!"

Says I, "I got one more here than I figured on. They called him Slim. You know him?"

He just nodded. "Slim Rainwater. A cousin."

Says I, "He got a reward on him too?"

The sheriff shook his head. "Not that I know of. Just Owen and Harvey. Slim never done anything much but tag along and drink bad whiskey."

I told the sheriff I was sorry to hear that. I hated to kill a man when there was no reason for it.

That seemed to strike him odd. He says, "If there'd been a reward, would you of felt better about killing him?"

I told him I would. A reward made a pretty good reason.

In such a case as that, when nobody knowed of any more family, it was customary to sell the horses and guns and saddles and such, and whatever was left over from the expenses of the burial was divided up by the sheriff amongst them he felt was entitled to it. In this case it was a fifty-fifty split between him and me. I never did see that he really had it coming to him, but it wasn't no big lot of money, and I had to depend on him to get me the reward for the Rainwater boys. I didn't feel like quibbling. Most of the sheriffs and marshals them days didn't draw much salary for the kind of job they did. A little extra money was always appreciated.

It taken me about ten or twelve days to get the reward because there wasn't no telegraph there, and the mail service wasn't none too peart. Meantime I just hung around town and played me some poker and taken a drink or two when I wanted it. I didn't sleep in the wagonyard no more, or fork hay. People came from a long ways to see Joe Pepper, the man who killed the Rainwater boys, and funny as it seems, I found this was good for business. They all seemed like they felt honored to get to play a hand of poker with Joe Pepper. I can't say as I favored their reasons much, but the main thing was the money. Taking them as a whole, they was a pretty miserable bunch of poker players. By the time the reward came in, I had cleaned up around there pretty good.

The sheriff came one day and says, "I got the authorization in today's mail. If you'll walk down to the bank with me, I'll see that you get paid."

It was a nice, refreshing walk. I enjoyed it a lot. I had already met the head man of the bank, a friendly old German by the name of Dietert. I had met his number-two man, too, a sour-faced, sour-tongued gink by the name of Clopton. Lord knows what *his* pedigree was.

I preferred old man Dietert myself. He had come out west from San Antonio a few years earlier and had established this bank and a mercantile and lumber and wool-buying and hide-buying business, and no telling what else that might turn him a dollar. He had sat in with me on a couple of games of poker at one of the saloons. He was good at handling money, all right, but he didn't have much knack for cards. I had thinned him a little. Them old Germans, they wouldn't play long enough to let you trim them to the quick. Some folks thought because they talked a little funny that they wasn't very smart, and that's how they generally bested you in business. They was thinking in two languages and out ahead of you in both of them.

Of course old man Dietert knowed what the letter was about; he had knowed it would be coming. But he read it over and looked at the draft real careful to be sure everything was in proper order. Them Dutchmen was always particular about proper order. He might make mistakes at the poker table, but he didn't make none at the bank. He says, "Vell, Mister Pepper, by the looks of this you're fifteen hundred dollars richer."

I told him that was the way I figured it, too.

He went on to tell me about the bank and how stable and safe it was and how fast the country was growing and how much bigger the bank was going to be in another five years. He suggested maybe I'd like to put my money there on interest and watch it grow with the bank. I told him I hadn't made plans to stay that long myself, and that I'd rather just get the cash money and go.

He said he was right sorry to hear that. He thought a man of my talents might find it profitable to stay around awhile and help out the sheriff. There was still some desperate sorts in the country who needed to meet up with Joe Pepper, and whose apprehension or demise was likely to be worth money to somebody, someplace.

The way he put it, I couldn't help but get to thinking. I wasn't going noplace special. Since the sheriff didn't already have my real name and description on a flyer, maybe he never would have; maybe they wasn't being mailed this far west. And even if one *did* come, there was a good chance I'd be the first to see it. It would be real easy to fold it up and shove it into the stove.

The banker's remark kind of taken the sheriff by surprise. I says, "What do you think about it, Sheriff?" I could already tell by the look on his face that he wasn't real keen on the notion. But the banker was a man of influence, because he taken on like he thought it was the best idea to come along since bourbon whiskey.

And that's how come Joe Pepper to wear a deputy sheriff's badge.

Chapter 4

It didn't take me long to learn some things about the sheriffing business, things that ain't wrote down in the statutes. Sheriff Smathers taken pains not to antagonize me about it, but he just the same let me know sort of kindly that the idea of me being a deputy was the banker's, not his. He had as soon I hadn't stayed because a feller like me tended to draw lightning, and he was getting to be an old man. He wasn't sure he could dodge fast enough when it struck. Another thing, since I was working out of his office and had his official stamp on me, so to speak, he said it was clear to him that any rewards I came up with ought to be divided with him, share and share alike. I didn't see his case quite as clear as he did, but I told him we would talk about it when the time came. His part of any split, I told him, ought to be calculated according to how much effort he put into the job, the chances that was taken, and such like. I've always been one that believed a man works best when he's got a proper incentive. Give him the same whether he works or sits down, and he'll wear out the seat of his britches before he wears out the knees.

There was some other things about sheriffing that came as a little of a surprise to me. There was some places around town that didn't operate strictly according to the statutes. There was laws that said it was illegal to gamble. There was laws about a saloon being open till way late at night or on a Sunday. And there was laws about them fancy houses down on Red Lantern Row. Most of them laws, I found out, was honored mainly in the breach. About once a week the sheriff made him a little round of all them places, and when he came back his pockets was fuller than when he left. You know as well as I do, that ain't the normal order of things with most folks that patronize them kinds of businesses.

If I'd of wanted to put the boot on the other foot I could of asked him to share that with me, same as he wanted me to share rewards. But at the time the thought of taking a percentage off of them poor unfortunate girls went against my grain. Being partial to the cards myself, I thought I could see the gamblers' side of it, too. Later on I learned better; I learned that the smart one takes what he can while the rest ponder Scripture. But wisdom ain't born in you; you got to cultivate it.

Catclaw was an agreeable kind of a town, once I got used to it. There was a little farming along close to the creek, but not enough of it to be any real setback to the community. People had a way of tending to their own affairs and not crowding in too much on other folks'. Big part of the town was Mexican, of course, and the sheriff being white, he didn't mess around much in the south part of town as long as the trouble there didn't spill over. The way he seen it them people had been keeping their own laws since long before the rest of us came. If a man was wronged, he taken it on himself to set things right. If a man was killed, his kin taken it on themselves to balance the books and take an eye for an eye. It wasn't anybody else's business, sure not the government's.

I used to wonder if that wouldn't be a good policy for us *gringos*, too. It would sure starve a lot of lawyers to death.

There wasn't much money to be made over in the Mexican section, which is another reason why Smathers didn't care to go over there. What little real money there was, it accumulated in the Anglo section. Texas was still dirt-poor. Main thing it had was land and cattle, and neither one of them worth real specie. They was hard times for us honest men, and none too easy for all them other folks. About the only actual money that had come into the state had been brought back by cattlemen taking their herds north, and by the carpetbaggers who had come in to steal everything that wasn't bolted down tight. No matter how hard they tried, they couldn't keep some of their money from getting into circulation.

The town had a fair to middling trade territory, selling goods to the ranchers and farmers and what-not on down to the Rio Grande on the south, way out into the edge of Apache country on the west, and north up to where there was nothing but Comanches. A couple of big general stores did business to the outlying country, and seven or eight saloons did business without having to go anywhere. Them days, no matter how hard the times, the last man to starve out was the saloonkeeper. When *he* left, you could take down the town sign.

There wasn't too many ways for people to move west without going through this town or some other one like it. Most of the people from San Antonio or points south had to come through unless they made it a point to leave the main road and go around. It was them roundance people I mostly kept a lookout for. I memorized all the "wanted" flyers, pretty near, and kept notes in a tally-book in my shirt pocket, the way

I've seen Texas Rangers do. One of them Rangers ever come upon a suspicious-looking bunch of strangers, he would take out his notebook and flip through it and check descriptions. If any looked like they might fit, he invited them to go with him. They hauled in a lot of the innocent along with the guilty, but one of them Ranger invitations was hard to refuse.

I made me a regular patrol north and south of town, cutting sign on people that taken the long way around. As scattered and few as the towns was, any man that taken pains to go around instead of coming through was naturally suspect. Biggest part of the time it was for nothing. Either I never would find them, or they would turn out to be Mexican cowboys looking for stock, or like once happened, some black troopers out of Fort Clark hunting for a couple of deserters. The Army was always asking us to help find these runaway boys, but I didn't feel like it was my place; them damn-yankees could hunt for their own. I felt like any soldier that had gumption enough to run was beginning to display some good sense.

Besides that, the Army didn't usually offer any reward.

Once in a while I would strike paydirt and catch me somebody that was on the dodge. Generally they would come peacefully enough, once I showed them the seriousness of my intentions. Getting them to town was only the first part of the trouble, like as not. Them upstanding citizens that put up reward money was always looking for some excuse not to pay it, once you done your part of the job. They would claim that the time had run out or that the reward wasn't meant for no regularly paid officer, or some such dodge, trying to rob an honest lawman of his due.

I remember one time I caught an old gotch-eared boy that had robbed a carpetbag bank in one of them settlements over east of San Antonio. They had put up a thousand dollars on him. It wasn't just that he had

robbed the bank which bothered them so much. He didn't really get off with much money. But afterwards he had taken the head banker for a hostage. He taken him along with him for maybe twenty miles, then made him strip off naked so he wouldn't be in no hurry to run to somebody's house for help. It's bad enough to lose your money, and even worse to lose your dignity on top of it.

Of course I didn't know the whole story when I went after him. All I knowed was what he looked like, and that part about the thousand dollars. The rest was just unnecessary details. I found him hiding out in the same general part of the country where Harvey Rainwater had been. I knowed him on sight; a man with a gotch ear just don't hardly melt into a crowd. I figured right off that he was a likable sort because he hadn't been there more than a couple of days, and he already had made friends that was willing to risk getting punctuated with my gun to protect him. But friendly don't count for much against a thousand dollars. I persuaded him, you might say, that he ought to come and go with me and not cause them new friends of his any undue grief. He came around to my point of view after I put a bullet through the fleshy part of his leg. I was kind of sorry about that later, seeing the way them people there made a fuss over him and patched him up so neat and fixed him a lunch to eat on the way to the jail. They didn't fix *me* nothing.

After he had time to get over the pain in that leg, and after the fever had run out, I could tell what the people seen in him. He had a grin wider than a pasture gate, and he could tell the biggest and funniest lies. If lies get a man sent to hell, I reckon he wouldn't have a chance. But they was healthy lies, the kind that make you laugh and don't hurt nobody. He asked for a guitar, and we brought him one. Worst guitar player you ever heard in your life.

Naturally I sent word back where he had come from

that we had him in jail, awaiting their pleasure. Well sir, they didn't lose much time getting theirselves over there . . . the county sheriff, a deputy, and the banker himself, a fat, whining kind of a Yankee. I knowed from what Gotch had told me that he was one of them carpetbaggers who had come down on us like a plague of locusts after the war, working in cahoots with their reconstruction laws to freeze people off of their land and then buy it up cheap for the delinquent taxes. He had cleaned out Gotch's family that way, which was why Gotch picked on him so. Gotch had told me all about walking that banker home, barefoot plumb to his chin, and I don't know which of us had laughed the hardest at the story.

The sheriff wasn't a bad sort, as them scalawag officeholders went, but that banker was one of them dollar-nursing kind that wouldn't spend two bits to watch a bumblebee whip a bald eagle. Soon as he seen we had his bank robber safely behind the bars, he crawfished on the reward. Said it had been for Gotch's capture within a month, and this had been two-going-on-three. I looked real close at that flyer. It didn't say a word about no time limit. He said it was supposed to have, and it was the printer's mistake, not his. If I wanted my thousand dollars, I would just have to take it up with the printer. I've seen enough printers in my time to know they're always broke.

On top of that, he had the nerve to ask us for the borrow of a horse that they could take Gotch home on.

I've been shot at in my life, and I've been cheated, and I believe I was always maddest at being cheated. I used the Lord's name in a shameful manner. It didn't change nothing. They still had the legal papers to take my prisoner, and they wasn't going to pay me a dime.

On top of that, I had come to like old Gotch. The truth wasn't in him, but neither was there any real harm.

They was going to leave at daylight the next morn-

ing. The banker had a hotel room. The sheriff and the deputy slept in the hay at the wagonyard because their county wasn't allowing them much in the way of expenses, and the banker sure wasn't paying. I sat in the front office, stewing over the situation and listening to Gotch abusing that Mexican guitar. All of a sudden it come to me. Gotch hadn't tried to shoot me when I taken him; he had just refused to go with me. I went in there and says, "Gotch, you ever shot a man in your life? You ever tried to?"

He said he hadn't. I says, "If somebody was to slip you a loaded pistol through that window, would you shoot that fat banker to get yourself free?"

He says, "No, I'd maybe try to scare him to death, but not shoot him."

There was maybe twenty pistols in a drawer that had been taken off of one man or another and never given back. I didn't get Gotch's because that would be a dead giveaway, and his wasn't much account anyway. If you're going out of your way to give a man something, you ought to give him something good. I picked me one and taken several cartridges and loaded it, then got to thinking. Now and again I'd been fooled about people. Maybe I oughtn't to take any undue chances. I taken the cartridges back out and pulled the lead from them, poured the powder into a spittoon and fitted the lead back in place. Then I reloaded the pistol with them, walked around back of the jail and rapped on the bars with the barrel. I seen a hand reach out, and I put the gun in it.

In a little while I heard Gotch playing on that guitar again.

I didn't go next morning to unlock the cell for that visiting sheriff and his deputy and the banker. I just gave them the key and told them I was going down the street to have me some breakfast. I seen that they had their horses, plus one they had had to buy at the wa-

gonyard for Gotch to ride. The liveryman owed me a split on that.

I walked down the street a ways, then ducked behind a corner where I could look back. Sure enough, I seen them three come out in single file with their hands up, and old Gotch bringing it up behind them with that pistol in his hand, grinning like a dog licking clabber. They rode out of town, heading west instead of east.

I went on and did what I had said I would . . . had me a thousand-dollar breakfast. It was one of the best meals I ever ate. Old Sheriff Smathers came around later in the morning, and I never let on to him.

Way after dark that night, the three of them came a-limping back into town sorefooted, all of them as naked as the day they first come into the world. And a whole lot smarter. They hadn't only lost their prisoner, but they had lost four head of horses and their guns and whatever cash and truck they had brought with them.

I think that banker suspicioned what had happened, because he tried awful hard to get me fired. But old Smathers wasn't keen on it, seeing as he would of shared the reward with me if there had been one. The banker finally offered to put up the reward again, a thousand dollars alive, two thousand dollars dead. But by then his welcome had plumb worn out. I told him it was a little like trapping coyotes. If you ever catch one in a trap and he gets loose, he's trap-wise from then on and ten times harder to catch. I wanted to hunt easier game.

That banker had to float a loan from old man Dietert at the Catclaw bank to buy them some clothes and horses.

I always had a hunch Smathers smelled a rat about Gotch, but he never said nothing. The only thing he ever wondered about was what happened to his spittoon. He pitched a smoked-down cigar butt in it and damn near caught his britches afire.

*   *   *

By and by I had added five or six rewards to my bank account, probably two or three thousand dollars in all. I still had it in my head that I wanted to be a rancher, even though all my attempts at it had come to considerable grief. That wasn't the part of the country I especially wanted to do it in, though. For one thing it was a heap dryer than the land I was used to, back home. It was really a lot better than it looked, I know now, but it always appeared to be in the midst of a drouth if you was from a greener part of the country. Another thing, I still figured they was looking for me back yonder, and sooner or later somebody might come straying through who knew me. I'd already had to leave a ranch in South Texas and another in Mexico. I didn't aim to leave one here.

Time came when one office seemed a little close for me and Sheriff Smathers. We come to something of a disagreement over a five-hundred-dollar reward on a feller that had shot a woman back in East Texas. Now, you're probably wondering how me, on the dodge myself, could go out and bring in other people on the dodge and keep my conscience clear. Truth is, I didn't. Like with old Gotch there; if I'd of turned him over to that fat banker and his laws, I'd of lost some sleep over it. I always hurt a little over most of them, and I couldn't of done it if money hadn't been such a cool balm for a troubled conscience.

One like that woman-killer, of course, didn't trouble me a bit except that he hadn't given me any excuse for shooting him. I always figured the best cure for a man like that is a deep burying. The reward was the same dead or alive.

Anyway, I had to catch him all by myself. I didn't get three cents' worth of help from old Smathers or anybody else. So when the reward came through, naturally I was inclined to figure I ought to keep it myself. Old Smathers seen it different. He wasn't overly strong at sharing danger, but he was real apt with pencil and paper when it come to sharing money.

Things didn't improve a bit when some old boy breezed into town one day and robbed our old Dutch banker in broad daylight. I was off at the time, looking for suspicious tracks on the trails south of town. First I heard of it was along late in the day when I was heading back toward town, tired and in bad need of a drink. I ran smack into a wild-eyed citizen posse, carrying more guns than Lee had at Gettysburg. You take the majority of them posses, they're more danger to each other than to the people they're hunting.

Feller in charge was that sour-faced loudmouth, Clopton, from the bank. I always figured he had a grand notion that one day he was going to be the high muck-a-muck in charge of all the money, when the old man died. He wasn't ever very civil, and that day none atall. He asked me if I didn't know the bank had been robbed, and of course that was a silly question because he knowed I'd been out of town.

He gave me a lecture about how a peace officer was supposed to be on hand when he was needed instead of out pleasure-riding around over the country, and I told him I was hot and thirsty and tired, and it had sure been no pleasure. Besides, bank robbers wasn't in the habit of making an appointment before they favored us with a visit.

I had been told that this Clopton was an officer in the Confederate Army, which didn't overly surprise me. It helped explain his extra airs, and some of the reason why we lost. He had been in the bank when the robber came in. Of course he didn't tell me all of it, but I found it out later when I finally got back into town. The robber was a youngish sort, no different from a hundred or two others you'd of met on the ranches and in the army and on the freight wagons. What Clopton didn't tell me was that the old banker Dietert stayed cool and just about had the robber bluffed into thinking the bank had sent nearly all of its cash out in a payroll. But Clopton was scared for his life, and he opened up the safe. The robber got off with maybe a thousand dollars in paper money; the silver was heavy, and he must not've wanted to get his horse loaded down. Clopton was afraid the boy would kill all of them when he got through, so as to leave no witnesses. When he left without doing anybody any harm, Clopton went and shut the safe—a little late to be doing that—and then went into a crying jag.

By the time I met him on the trail he was over it, and he was talking and acting tough. He was probably trying to make up for the show he had put on earlier.

The robber had come south; they generally did them days, because it wasn't far to Mexico. Clopton said if I'd had my eyes open I was bound to've seen him. But I hadn't seen anybody all day except a couple of Mexican oxcart men and a little detail of them black soldiers out of Fort Clark with a consumptive-looking white lieutenant who probably *needed* to rob a bank.

There wasn't nothing I could do but turn around with that posse and help them hunt. It was a big rolling country of mesquite and catclaw and *guajillo* and all that other half-desert kind of growth that could swallow a man up with you looking straight at him. We cut for signs but didn't find any. Sheriff Smathers had gone out with another posse, in a little different direction. I found out that the boy had managed to cover his trail just a little ways out of town, and nobody could tell where he went to.

We hunted till full dark. By then I was glad it was a town posse, because they was all ready to turn around and go home. One of them *serious* posses, now, they'd of stayed out two or three days without a bite to eat. I wasn't ready to do that, not for an amateur robber who hadn't gotten off with but a thousand dollars and hadn't shot anybody.

I changed my tune when I found out what else got

taken. I went down to the bank early next morning to see if old man Dietert could give me a better description than that idiot Clopton. I found the old Dutchman busy trying to convince several people that their money was still safe, that he would stand good for any loss out of his own personal pocket. But for me he had to make an exception.

"I'm sorry to tell you this," he says, "but you vill remember that leather pouch you vanted me to keep in the safe? It is gone."

Well sir, I couldn't help cussing a little. I had almost got myself killed getting hold of that gold in the first place. And I had had to take it away from a thief and kill him. I swear, it began to look like the good Lord didn't intend for me to have it.

The cash money I had on deposit was all right, but it sure made me sick to lose that gold pouch again after all the trouble I had been to.

I didn't wait around for anybody to form up a fresh posse. I set out by myself. But it was too late to pick up that old boy's trail. There had been so many people riding around over that country looking for him that it was hopeless. I rode on south, all the way to the river, hoping to pick up some kind of a clue. I found lots of tracks, but there was no way of knowing which one of them might be his, or if any of them was. I brewed it over in my mind for a long time before I finally got up nerve to cross that river into Mexico. I had thought once that I'd seen enough of Mexico to do me for a lifetime. But I decided to take the risk. This was so far upriver that they had probably never heard of Santos, much less of Joe Peeler.

I hunted around down there for several days, looking over all the suspicious characters. Just about every *gringo* I seen that was past seventeen looked suspicious, the frame of mind I was in. About all I had to go on was the description of the horse, a smallish mustang-type bay with a little streak on his nose. I must of found a hundred like that, but no *gringo* riding any of them. I finally gave it up and went back across the river where I belonged, tired out and feeling low. I wasn't ready for the griping of old Sheriff Smathers. He was saying I must be turning lazy, that I ought to've stayed down there till I found the robber because by this time the bank had put up a five-hundred-dollar reward on him.

He sure hated it, not getting a cut of that reward. But he didn't hate it half as bad as I did, because he hadn't lost a sack of gold coin that he had become attached to.

He kept grousing, and it was a pleasure to get out of town again. I kept on for awhile working that country between town and the river, not getting nothing for it but a saddlesore.

That old boy was gone, and there was nothing to do but accept it. The hell of it was, I was the biggest loser of anybody in town.

Chapter 5

One thing about me, I could always tell when the gravy was running thin. I knew my time in Catclaw was about up. It was getting so every time old Smathers opened his mouth, I had to open mine too. The strain between us got considerable. He would of loved to've sat in the office and watched me bring in the feller who taken the bank, so he could share in the reward. But some games are meant to be won and some are meant to be lost. That time we had a busted flush.

It was a good thing for me, I guess, that Samantha Ridgway came along when she did.

Actually she came the second time before I chanced to see her. I was off on one of them wild goose chases when she first came through with one of them little emigrant wagon trains that seemed to pass there about as regular as a man washed his socks. It wasn't a big one like you read about, the kind with a hundred wagons. There wasn't ever as many of that kind as folks seem to think, at least not down in our part of the country. Most of the time they was more like five or six, maybe eight or ten wagons. Those was the easiest managed. The folks in the front wagon could always look back and see the hindmost, and vice versa. The last ones didn't eat near as much dust as on a big train. An outrider could see the fore and aft wagons all at the same time and knowed right away when anything went wrong.

Oft as not when you came onto one of them little wagon trains, you found a lot of people was kinfolks. I always had a fondness for families myself, growing up in a big one the way I did.

Like I say, I missed Samantha the first time. If it hadn't been for some Apaches off out to the west, she would of never left any footprints on my life. The wagons camped at the edge of town one night while the folks picked up some supplies, then headed west toward old Fort Davis, way off out across the Pecos River country.

This, you got to understand, was before Mackenzie made his big cavalry raid out of Fort Clark and tore up the worst nest of them border-jumping Indians in northern Mexico. These Indians would stay in Mexico most of the time because the Mexicans was too busy with problems of their own to bother them much. Now and again they would cross the river, hit somebody with some devilment, then not let their breechclouts touch them till they was safe south of the Rio Grande. Mexico didn't care much, seeing a bunch of *Tejanos* get bloodied up.

Well sir, this emigrant train never made it to the Pecos. Them Indians came skinning out from behind one of the flat-topped mountains you find in that desert country, and before the folks could get the wagons circled the red devils was amongst them. Things got fiercesome for a few minutes till the Apaches took what they mainly wanted, the loose horses and mules. They would always kill a few people if it came handy, but the stock was the main thing.

When the dust cleared, the emigrants had three men to bury out on that greasewood flat. Before they could get back to town they had to stop and bury another one.

I was west of Catclaw a few miles, scouting around for suspicious sign, when I met a feller pushing his horse pretty hard, heading east. He asked me how much farther it was to Catclaw, and I told him. "Thank God," he says, and points back over his shoulder. "There's a wagon train behind me needing help. There any doctors in the town?"

I told him there was two, one *gringo* and one Mexican. Told him to get the Mexican because he didn't drink much. He allowed as they would need them both.

He went on toward town, and I followed the mail road west till I came finally to the wagons. A more desperate, hard-whipped bunch I never seen. Not only did they lose their loose stock, but the Indians killed some more in the traces. That was the way with the Indian when he went to war: kill what he couldn't steal, and leave the white man afoot if he couldn't leave him dead. So these people had to double up with what stock they had left. They even doubled some of their wagons in tandem, one behind the other like freight wagons. The wagon canvas was shot full of holes, and a couple was partly burned. They was a confused and staggered lot of people, I'll tell you. Some people went west them days that shouldn't of ever left hearth and home.

It was Samantha that caught my eye, sitting up on a wagonseat, driving the wagon all by herself. She wasn't a lot to look at just at the time, I'll grant you, but somehow she sort of grabbed me. Her face was smudged with dirt and ashes. There was streaks down her cheeks where the tears had run. Her hair was all blowed out and wild-looking. But with all of that, she taken my breath.

I says to her, "You're kind of small to be driving that team all by yourself. You need some help?"

She says, "My mother's the one that needs help. You a doctor?"

I told her I wasn't. I stood up in the stirrups and looked into the wagon. A woman was lying in there on a pile of blankets, white and pale as if death was knocking on her door. And it was. A big middle-aged woman was sitting in there with her, holding onto her hand.

As things unfolded, I found out that her husband had been more or less the captain of the wagon train, a family leader and all that. He had been out front trying to get the wagons circled when the Indians hit, and he was the first one to get killed. The old lady— Samantha's mama—went running out to try and help him. She grabbed up his rifle and tried to fire it, but it was empty. She swung it like a club till one of them put a bullet in her.

They was a strong, loyal bunch of women them days, preacher, not like them little bicycle-riding, croquet-playing dolls you see around nowadays. Why, just a little while back I even seen a woman smoking a cig- arette . . . a *cigarette*, mind you . . . and she was sup- posed to be a lady, not a saloon girl. Some people these days don't know the first thing about morals.

But that's got nothing to do with what I'm telling you. I rode back to the lead wagon. A big, stocky farmer was sitting there on it, looking grim as death. And he had plenty to be grim about. I found out his name was Zebulon Wentworth. They was great on Bi- ble names in them days. Of course the ones that knowed him called him Zeb, which kind of took the Bible back out of it. Zebulon was for Sunday, like the Bible generally is.

Old Zeb's wife was a sister to Samantha's mother, and now people looked to him to head up the wagon train. He was one of them tough East Texas farmers that had spent so long behind a plow that his hands was shaped to fit the handles. Big hands, like a ham hanging up in a smokehouse. He could knock a man rolling if he was of a mind to, though generally him and his kind had no such inclinations.

He asked me if I had met his man on the road. Then he told me they had had some trouble, which I could plainly see for myself. But I reckon he needed somebody new to talk to, because he commenced telling me all about the Indian raid. I found out that the big woman sitting with the wounded lady back in that other wagon was his wife Addie. Zeb was sore afraid he was fixing to lose his sister-in-law. He was telling me how hard that was going to be on his niece Samantha, both of her folks getting killed and leaving her to shift for herself, a young and innocent girl of nineteen, facing the cruel world. My heart kind of weakened as I listened to him.

By and by I could see a bunch of horses coming. Old Zeb tensed up like he thought it might be Indians again, but I told him it was likely a bunch from town, coming to meet them. And that's what it turned out to be. That Mexican doctor was in the lead with a black bag tied on behind his saddle. The *gringo* doctor couldn't come, somebody said, but he would be waiting when the wagons got to town. I'd seen a good bit of him since I had been in Catclaw, and I figured somebody was getting him sobered up.

They stopped the wagons so the *medico* could look at the wounded. He started with Samantha's mother. She was fevered and talking out of her head. I had seen enough wounded men in the war to know that she didn't stand much chance. The doctor must of knowed it too, but he didn't tell the folks so. He looked at her pretty good, then went to the other wagons. There was two men wounded, and one little boy that got a broken arm by falling out of a wagon while the fight was going on. They wasn't in any big danger of dying unless it was from embarrassment because of so many of them people from town, crowding around looking at them.

The doctor went back to Samantha's wagon. He told Samantha and her aunt Addie and Zeb that old lady Ridgway was in a bad fix, and that the bullet needed to come out of her right away. He hated to do it there, but he was afraid to wait till they could get to town. So we spread some blankets on the ground in the shade under the wagon, and unhitched the team so they couldn't spook and accidentally run the wheels over her. I helped a couple of men lift her down from the wagon and put her on the blankets. Then the doctor shooed all the extra folks away so there wouldn't be a bunch of people watching when he opened up her dress. He kept me and Zeb there to help him, and of course three or four of the women. He didn't have anything to put her to sleep, so he gave her all the laudanum he thought was safe. Then he commenced.

I watched that girl while the operation was going on. She stood back out of the way. The tears ran down through the dust on her face, but she didn't let out a whimper or break down and get to be a problem like lots of women would've done. She had her head down some, praying. I thought to myself how lucky that woman was to have such a daughter.

I see people nowadays who get more loyalty out of a yellow dog than out of their kids, but there I go talking about things that have nothing to do with the story.

We had to hold Mrs. Ridgway tight because it hurt her. That bullet was in there solid. The worst part was that it had already been in too long. By and by the doctor finally brought it out. Old Zeb gave a sigh of relief, and his big wife Addie said, "Thank God," but I knowed from the look in that Mexican doctor's face that it had all been for nothing.

The poor woman had fainted from the pain, and I personally had some doubt that she would ever come to. The doctor got the blood stopped and the wound taken care of the best he could. We put the lady back into the wagon, and the train started moving again toward Catclaw.

A big lot of people had gathered to watch the wagons come in. I pointed Zeb toward a big open piece of camping ground next to the wagonyard.

There was one thing about people in them days: They might quarrel and raise hell amongst theirselves, but when trouble came most of them was there to help each other. Being summer, the schoolhouse was empty. A bunch of people had already rushed over and fixed the place up to make a kind of hospital out of it. The woman teacher normally stayed in a little room in the back, where there was a stove and a bed and dresser and such. The women in town had already fixed this up for Mrs. Ridgway to give her some privacy. Cots had been brought in and set up for the wounded men and the boy in the main schoolroom. The benches and tables was shoved back against the wall.

They had the *gringo* doctor sobered up pretty good, but his hands was still shaking. I was glad the Mexican had already done the operation on Mrs. Ridgway because folks would of naturally chosen the *gringo* doctor over him. That would of been a bad mistake.

Like I said, people was good to pitch in and help where they could. The liveryman over at the wagonyard had all the people's stock brought into one of his corrals, and he put out hay for them. Said he wouldn't let the people pay him for it. Later on I figured out that he already sensed he was going to get to sell these folks a bunch of horses and mules to make up for the ones that the Indians had killed or got off with. That would make a little hay look cheap. But maybe what he done was all out of the kindness of his heart; it ain't for me to say it wasn't.

The wagon people made camp but didn't have to cook supper. People from the town kept coming out, bringing them stuff. I circulated amongst the wagon folks, talking to the ones that felt like talking. I found out that most of them was kin. They had come out of the old colonies of deep East Texas. The carpetbaggers had taxed them out of most of what they owned, and they was going west for a new start. They had heard farming land could be had cheap along the Rio Grande west of El Paso. They had elected Samantha's pa to head up the bunch. He had never done no Indian-fighting, but he had stood up against his share of Yankees in the war. He knowed a man's duty.

After he was killed, folks naturally looked to old Zeb Wentworth to lead them. He hadn't been off to war, but he had been in the home guards. He was there when the Yankees tried to invade Texas by way of Sabine Pass and got the pants shot off of them. I watched him there at the wagon, going around to the folks to be sure they all got camped all right, seeing that the stock was all cared for. I knowed he would of rather been down at the schoolhouse with his wife, seeing after his sister-in-law and his niece.

There might of been a lot he didn't know about westering, but he had the nerve to give it a good try. He had the look of a mild and gentle man, and mainly that's what he was. But one of the wagon people told me something that made me study him closer. Seems like the carpetbaggers and scalawags wasn't content to just take the land away from these people, but they tried to stop the wagon train and take away what little else they still had, claiming it was due on back taxes. One carpetbagger made a bad mistake, though. He laid his hands on a woman, trying to make her open a big wooden trunk so he could see if there was any money in it. In just the time it taken him to fall, he was laying on his back with a big hole between his eyes, and old Zeb was standing there with a rifle smoking. The rest of them thieves ran as fast as they could, back to the county seat.

That's the kind of people them farmers was. They minded their own business and was no worry to anybody except those that tried to mess with them.

It stood to reason there was probaby a reward out for Zeb back where he came from. But *I* wasn't tempted to do anything about it, not a particle.

I went up to Zeb finally and asked him if there wasn't something more I could do to help. He said if I wasn't a minister and wasn't a doctor, he guessed not. I had helped patch up a few wounded in my time, but I sure wasn't no minister.

I says to him, "What'll you-all do now? You're too crippled to go on."

He looked at me like he didn't understand what I said. He says, "We're crippled, but we ain't all dead. Sure we'll go on. We ain't finished what we set out to do."

That was their way; if there had just been one of them left alive, he would of gone on for the rest of them, or died making the try.

I rode down to the schoolhouse with him, partly because I knowed I'd see that girl and partly because something about this old man and his tribe had sort of got to me. I noticed that the first thing Zeb done when he walked in the door was to take his hat off, like it was a church or somebody's house, instead of just an empty school. His eye was on the door to the room where his own closest family was, but first he went to the wounded men and the boy and inquired after their health.

Samantha heard his voice and came out the door. She shut it behind her, kind of a sign that it was closed to the public in there. Real gentle, old Zeb asked her how her mother was. She didn't say anything; she just kind of answered him with her eyes.

All that time I had been trying to figure what it was about her that had hit me so hard. All of a sudden I knew. She reminded me of my Millie, my lost Millie. She was just about Millie's size and build, and with her face all smudged up like it was with dirt and grime and soot, the differences didn't show. Even her eyes was like Millie's.

She was, right at first, like Millie come back to me alive.

By the time I finally seen her with her face clean, and could tell she was a whole different woman, it didn't matter anymore. I was hooked tighter than a catfish on a trotline.

The old man hugged her, which I would of loved to of done, but of course that was unthinkable. I'd of wound up like that carpetbagger, trying to see out through a third eye. And I'd of had it coming to me.

Sometime during the night Samantha's old mother just drifted away in her sleep. Looking for her husband, I reckon. She never came back. Next afternoon they buried her in the town cemetery, over on the side with the "good" folks, away from all the hardnoses who had died wearing their boots. I'd have to say for the credit of the town that just about everybody turned out. Even the saloons closed. Not a soul there had knowed her, but they all done her honor. They went up on the hill after the hearse and sang about amazing grace and the blood of the lamb, and a few of the womenfolks cried like she was an old friend. They done right by her.

Samantha wished her mother could of been buried with her pa, but that wasn't practical. Old lady Addie told her they would find each other in Heaven; it didn't make much difference where they laid the clay.

Well sir, I kind of appointed myself an unofficial guardian and assistant to Zeb Wentworth. I made out like I figured it was my duty as a law officer. Mainly what it done was to give me a chance to see a right smart of that girl.

One thing was clear to me: These folks couldn't start out again the way they was, weakened so much. They had lost four men and a woman. It was going to be a few days before the two wounded men ought to have

to suffer the hardship of the trip. Besides, they needed
to heal up some so they could help if things came to
another bad pinch. I told Zeb if he would wait a few
days maybe there'd be some more emigrant wagons
come along to reinforce them. A man might make
twenty trips across that desert and not see an Indian.
Then, on the twenty-first trip, one would raise up from
behind a little greasewood bush and take his hair. It
was all a matter of chance. The Indians came and went
like the weather, and didn't leave many tracks.

All this time Sheriff Smathers was plaguing me
about that bank robber. Even if I caught him and got
the reward, after I split with old Smathers I wouldn't
have but two-fifty for my trouble. By then I was interested in something worth a lot more than any two-fifty.
I wanted that girl. So I spent most of my time with the
wagon people.

I didn't intrude myself on her or nothing, you understand; I just made it a point to always be around,
so that if she needed anything she didn't have to call
on nobody else.

The waiting was bad for me in one way, though,
because it gave the town women time to get acquainted
with the train women and swap gossip. You know how
women will talk. Some of their opinions of me wasn't
near as good as the opinion I had of myself. Well,
that's natural. People sometimes need a hard man to
do their fighting for them, and take the worst of the
risks for them, but he don't fit in with parlor society,
or even front-porch society. He stands outside someplace, needed too much to turn loose of but not enough
to bring him into the family. It's like they're never
quite sure of him, afraid maybe he'll go bad on them
one day. It's happened, plenty of times.

You'll often find that the man doing the hunting is
more like the man he's after than like the people that
pay him to do the job.

The wagon people wasn't loaded down with specie,

but they had enough cash for the absolute necessaries. Main thing they needed was some extra draft animals to take the place of the ones they had lost. The people in town was friendly enough and sympathetic, but they was like most folks . . . when it comes to business, friendship don't cross over.

During the time I had been at Catclaw, traveling around looking out for the snorty breed, I'd got to know a lot of the ranchers. I thought I knowed some who might have horses and mules they would sell cheaper than the wagonyard operator and the folks in town was asking. A couple of the wagon folks needed oxen, and I had gotten acquainted with enough Mexicans to know where some such could be had. So I went wih Zeb Wentworth and a couple of others, trying to help them spend where the dollar was biggest.

Naturally that left some of the townfolks thinking sour thoughts about me, and speaking sour words. The keeper of the wagonyard had seemed like a pretty good friend of mine, but he cooled off after I done him out of the sale of twelve horses and mules. I figured he wasn't hurt none. There would be plenty of wagon folks coming through after these was gone, needing stock to replace some that went lame or died along the way. I wouldn't care if he stuck *them*, but these was *my* wagon people.

Doing this little chore gave me a chance to get these wagon folks on my good side—the men, anyway—and maybe offset what some of the town people might be telling them. Of course the people in Catclaw didn't know nothing about me except what I had done while I was there. They didn't even know Joe Pepper wasn't my real name. But some of the women told Addie Wentworth that I was now and again seen down on Red Lantern Row in broad daylight, where a respectable man wouldn't go except in the dark of the night. They told her I was a man who went out and hunted people down for money, like a wolfer killing varmints for the bounty, as if that was a bad thing. The men I went after was always somebody they wanted to get rid of anyway.

Each family on the wagon train done its own cooking. Since Samantha was alone now, Zeb and Addie taken her under their wing. They was her closest kin, so it was the Christian thing to do. The old lady always seemed like she went out of her way to keep Samantha busy when I came around. She said it helped keep the girl's mind off of her grief. I figured it was to keep her mind off of *me*, if she had been thataway inclined.

I didn't try to press her. I just always tried to be somewhere close in case she needed somebody to talk to. I never tried putting my arm around her or kissing her when she wasn't expecting it, or stuff like that. I had a notion that would scare her off. I had intentions toward that girl, and they was all honorable.

I started dropping suggestions to Zeb that it looked like they was going to need some extra men to go with them. I didn't volunteer, exactly; I thought it would look better if he asked me instead of it being the other way around. And I figured that if I played the cards careful and easy, he would do it. Old Zeb and Samantha was alike in some ways. I could tell they both liked me.

But not Addie Wentworth. A more suspicious old woman you'd never find. She could see through me like a pane of window glass. Every time me and Samantha was about to strike up a conversation, the old woman thought of some chore that wouldn't wait, and she'd put Samantha on it. Then she would give me a look that would turn sweet milk into clabber. I tried to take it kindly and tell myself she was just interested in Samantha's welfare, same as I was, but I couldn't help wishing sometimes it had been *her* that got in the way of the Indians.

She was a hefty sort of a woman. Two or three times when I watched her climbing into her wagon, I almost let the devil talk me into pushing her just to see how hard she would fall. Of course I never actually done it, but thinking about it was pleasuresome.

She kind of taken me by surprise one day. Another time I might of told her off, but Samantha was there and I couldn't afford to say anything she might take bad. The old lady bored a pair of holes through me with her eyes. She says, "People tell me you're a gun-fighter who kills for money."

She caught me on my left foot, so to speak. All I could do for a minute was stammer. Finally I says, "I never shot no man that wasn't looking at me, and never one that didn't need it."

She didn't let up. She says, "I suppose you always considered that you did the world a favor."

I hadn't thought of it in quite that way. Any time I ever done a thing like that, the notion of doing the world a favor was a long ways from my thinking. I says, "I never been one to brag. But yes, I expect the world is better off without the ones I've put away."

I taken a long look at Samantha. I couldn't tell that I'd hurt myself in her sight. But I sure hadn't helped myself with old Addie.

It was pretty soon decided that the wounded was in shape to travel. And along about that time there come two more sets of wagons. One was some emigrant wagons with white folks. The other was a bunch of them old big-wheeled Mexican carts, traders headed out for El Paso with goods come all the way from ships that unloaded at the mouth of the Rio Grande. Naturally when the settlers on that mover train heard what the first wagon train had run into, they wasn't hard to talk into all joining together for the trip across the Pecos River country and out into the Davis Mountains, and then on to El Paso. There was a little discussion about maybe they could get along without the Mexicans. Some of the emigrants didn't know nothing about Mexicans except that they remembered the Alamo. But old

Zeb asked me and I told him they wasn't *marrying* the Mexicans, they was just traveling with them. That kind of tickled the old man; he always loved a joke.

I suppose I had planted enough seed so that the idea seemed to sprout in Zeb's head all by itself. He comes up to me after having a powwow with men from the other wagons, and he says, "Anything keeping you here, Joe?"

I acted like I didn't know what he was getting at. He told me flat out that he'd be pleasured if I was to come and go along with them. He had a notion I could be of help to them in that wild country. I told him I never had been out that way very far, and I didn't know the trail. I had played enough good poker that I figured my eyes wouldn't show how much I really wanted to go. I wanted them folks to figure it was all their own doing, so they would feel grateful to me instead of it having to be the other way around.

Zeb told me they had some maps that was supposed to be reliable, and he figured the trail had been beaten out so well that we wasn't apt to get lost. Main thing he wanted me for was as a guard, to help be sure they didn't get slipped up on again.

I told him I sure did feel bad about having to leave Sheriff Smathers, him depending on me so much. That was all a poker bluff, of course. Far as I was concerned old Smathers could go soak his head in a trough till he quit bubbling. He had about wore out his welcome with me.

I told Zeb I didn't have a wagon. He said it was better that way. They wanted me to be an outrider, a scout. A wagon would be in my way. "We can't afford to pay you," he says, "but you can take your meals at my wagon with me and Addie and Samantha. Addie'll be right tickled."

I figured Addie would only be tickled to feed me some ground-up glass. But the idea of sharing a campfire with Samantha made the whole thing sound fine.

Zeb still thought he was the fisherman. I didn't intend to let him suspicion that he was the fish. He says, "When we get out yonder to the valley, I expect there'll be farmland enough that you can get a share for yourself. We'll be pleased to have you for a neighbor."

I could still remember my boyhood pretty good. One thing I didn't share with these emigrants was their feeling for the plow. But I had begun to picture me having a ranch out there, with cattle running all over the hills, and a little ranchhouse with Samantha in it, fixing my supper every night. So I told Zeb if they really felt like they needed me, I'd make the sacrifice and settle up my affairs in town.

Old Smathers had already sensed that I wasn't long for that place. He didn't act very pleased when I laid the badge on his desk, but he didn't seem surprised none either. He says, "Throwing in with them farmers, are you? Anybody can tell by looking at you that you ain't no farmer. Maybe you figure you can get ahold of their money somehow."

That was about what I had expected of him. He always thought of everything in terms of money. I didn't tell him about Samantha because she wasn't none of his business, and he wouldn't of understood anyhow. He was long past the point where a good-looking woman stirred him up much.

I went over to the bank to draw my money. Old man Dietert seemed like he was sorry to see me go, especially since I was pulling a right smart of cash out of his safe. He told me how risky it was to carry all that cash around and offered to write me a draft on a bank out in El Paso. I told him no thanks. I knowed what to do about a man that tried to rob me with a gun, but it wasn't so easy to keep a man from robbing you with pen and ink. I was looking at Clopton when I said it, just being sure he got the message clear. The old man was all right, but one of these days he was going to die of his infirmities, and this town would be at the mercy of Clopton.

I got me a moneybelt and put all that money in it where it belonged, just under my heart.

The next morning at daylight we pointed them wagons west. There I was, way out yonder with a whole train of farmers, standing in some danger of contamination. You know what a wagon scout is, don't you? He's a fool who rides way out in front of everybody and says to the Indians, "Here I am, come get me." Of course he hopes there ain't none of them around to take up the invitation.

Well, there wasn't, not for a while. The wagon people was pretty tense for the first two or three days, till we got to where the battle had taken place. They sure didn't let the wagons stretch out much; they had the lead horses or mules of every team sticking their noses over the tailgate of the next wagon. Zeb hadn't figured to stop at the battle site, but it was late in the day, and everybody just naturally quit. There was fresh graves out there, and they wanted to pray over them one more time, since it wasn't likely any of these people would ever pass this way again. I think Zeb was more worried over the state of mind this would put them in than over the time they might be losing.

It was an awful quiet supper. Afterwards Samantha got up and started walking real slow out to where her father was buried. I went to follow her, but old Addie stepped in front of me. "She'll want to be alone," she warns me, meaning that *Addie* wanted her to be alone.

"I won't bother her," I says. "I'll just go out there and make sure no Indian slips up and joins her."

I just stood back and watched her. I could see her shoulders shake a little and knowed she was crying, and I wanted to go up and take her and hold her so bad I couldn't hardly stand it. But I knowed old Addie was watching from over by the wagons, and she would be out there like a hornet. Finally Samantha says, "You'd of liked him, Joe."

I told her I knowed I would've, which was likely true. I liked Zeb, and from what I could hear, Samantha's father had been cut out of the same timber.

She says, "It scares me, going on out yonder alone."

If she had any doubt before how I felt about her, I didn't leave her any. I says, "You ain't alone. If I have anything to do about it, you ain't ever going to be."

I don't know what I expected her to say to that. Maybe I thought she would come and fall into my arms. She didn't. She just turned and looked at me, and I couldn't read what was in her eyes. She smiled, just a touch, and she says, "I know that, Joe." And then she walked back toward the wagon.

As far as I was concerned, I had asked her to marry me. She hadn't said *no*, but she sure hadn't said *yes*, either.

We went on and never seen so much as a moccasin print. We had a little scare one day when a bunch of horsemen showed up in the distance, and we got all the wagons and carts circled in a hurry. The riders, though, turned out to be a patrol of black troopers with a white lieutenant working out of Fort Clark. They was on their way in after a hundred-mile scout, and they hadn't seen a thing.

People began to get so relaxed and confident that a few even quit being nice to the Mexican freighters. Decided, I reckon, that they wasn't going to need them after all.

Nighttimes, when I could talk to Samantha after supper where her old aunt couldn't hear us, I'd point out to her that a young woman all by herself that way couldn't take up a farm. It was by way of trying to get her to say she would step into double harness with me. But she would always say the Lord would show her the way when the time came; she figured He had plans for her.

I sure had plans for her.

I never did get to talk to her very long at a time. That old Addie seemed like she had twelve eyes, and half of them in the back of her head. She wouldn't give the two of us much chance for any real serious conversation.

Once when the old lady was busy digging through a trunk in her wagon and wasn't watching us, I got Samantha out and we started for a walk around the wagon circle in the moonlight. We hadn't got fifty yards before I heard somebody come trotting up behind us. I had my pistol out before I had time even to think about it. When I spun around I seen the old lady catching up to us. She didn't pay any more attention to that pistol than if it had been a matchstick. She says to Samantha, "You better get back to the wagon, sugar. It's dangerous out here."

Samantha says, "There ain't any Indians."

The old lady tried her best to kill me with a look from them two hard eyes. She says, "All the danger ain't from Indians."

Samantha done as she was told and started for her own wagon. The old lady hung back. When Samantha was out of hearing she turned on me like a mad cow hooking a wolf away from her calf. She says, "The rest of them don't see through you, Joe Pepper, but *I* do. You're trying to turn the head of a poor little orphan girl."

I pointed out to her that Samantha wasn't a little girl.

"She ain't old enough yet to know her own mind," Addie says. "Till she is, I'll help do her thinking for her. And *you* have no place in my thinking."

I didn't have anything but the best of motives in mind for that girl. I wasn't going to do a thing till the words had been properly read to us out of the Book. But I knowed there wasn't no use trying to convince Addie of that fact. I figured I would just keep working on Samantha, kind of slow and easy, and maybe by the time we got to El Paso I'd have her in a frame of mind to run off and look for a preacher with me. *That* would fix the old woman.

It was the next day, or the day after that, when Pete Ogden showed up.

I was way out in front of the wagons, kind of edging over toward some flat-topped mountains. We kept the wagons as far back from the mountains as we could because it was a favorite stunt of the Indians to hide till the wagons got to the closest point, then come charging and catch the wagons strung out. I worked over fairly close, but not so close that they wouldn't have theirselves one dandy horserace trying to catch me.

That's when I seen the Indians, coming at me through the greasewood, running hard. One looked like he was a good ways out in front.

First thing I done was fire my pistol into the air three times to let them wagon folks know they was fixing to have a visitation. Then I put spurs to that Santos black and figured to see just how fast he could really run. He was even better than I figured. He had seen them other horses coming at us, and I reckon he sensed that I was some excited. Horses have got a way of knowing. If it had been a matched race on some country track, we could of taken the whole pot.

The farmers didn't waste no time. When I got to the wagons they had already circled up and put all the loose stock inside. They had left a little gap for me to ride through, was all. The second I loped in, they pushed the wagons up tight.

I had left them Indians like they was caught in the quicksand. But the odd thing was that one man was still way out in front of the others. It finally struck me that he wasn't with them; they was chasing him. And he was coming for the wagons as fast as he could travel.

Old Zeb hollers, "That's a white man!"

Sure enough, I could tell now that he was wearing a hat, something the Indians hadn't commenced doing at the time. And under that hat was a wad of hair he was fixing to lose. His horse was giving out under him.

Samantha all of a sudden got to remembering seeing her father shot down in front of her eyes. She started hollering, "Somebody save him!"

I tried to tell her that anybody who went out there might not come back. I didn't feel like going out and risking my life to save a fool. It was damned obvious that the man was a fool or he wouldn't of been out there by himself in the first place. But she wasn't listening to that kind of argument. She was hollering for somebody to do something, and then she grabbed a rifle and started out there herself.

Way I seen it, that man could take care of himself or take what was coming to him, but I wasn't just about to let that girl get herself killed for some stranger. I ran out and grabbed her. I turned her around and pushed her back toward the wagon. Then I dropped to one knee and started shooting past the man, into that bunch of Indians. At the distance I couldn't do them any great damage, but maybe I was looking good to Samantha. In a minute several other men came out afoot and joined me, and we all started walking to meet the rider, shooting our rifles as we went.

The Indians kind of wavered at all that fire. I don't think we was hitting any of them, but we had sure got their attention. The rider was in a pretty fair way to make it, then, but his horse went down. He was still out there a hundred yards or so past us, afoot. That gave the Indians a last chance, and it looked for a minute like they was going to get him. Old Zeb got up and started running out to meet him. I couldn't do no less with that girl watching, so I jumped up and followed after him. A couple of the Mexicans was right up beside me, and one or two of the farmers. I suppose I'd

of looked better to Samantha if I'd been out in the lead.
But I'd always believed that the Lord helps them that
help theirselves, and I couldn't see where I was helping
myself much out there so far from the wagons. Not
with a dozen or fifteen Indians out there looking mad.

That feller was coming in to meet us even faster than
we was going out to meet him. The Indians had stopped
out there a ways and was taking potshots. Only three
or four had rifles, and it was way too far to send an
arrow. One of them got lucky and put a bullet in that
feller's leg. He went down like he had been hit with
an ax. He got up again, cussing like a politician who
has just lost the election. You'd of thought, after the
narrow escape he had, that he would of been more
considerate of the Lord's feelings. He kind of hopped
on his good leg and went down again.

Zeb hollered for him to lay still, that we was coming.
But he kept right on crawling and scrambling toward
us on his hands and knees, still looking back over his
shoulder. A man don't rightly respect fear, I suppose,
till he's had a bunch of Indians breathing on the back
of his neck.

He was in a right smart of a panic when we got to
him. I thought he was going to fight us right at first,
like he couldn't tell for sure if we was Indians. I told
him if he didn't behave himself I was going to stomp
him a little. I grabbed him under one arm and a Mexican grabbed him under another. We lit out with him
toward the wagons. Zeb and the others followed along
behind us, walking and running backwards, keeping
their eyes on the Indians. I was too busy to look, but
I was satisfied they kept edging on in toward us till we
got them up to good rifle range of the wagons. Then
they stopped.

As we got to the wagons I turned for a quick look.
I seen one of them Indians a hundred yards away. I
didn't know much about sign language, but I got the
gist of what he was telling us. The wagon people

started shooting at him, and he decided to leave.

We laid the feller down in the shade of a wagon. He was groaning and cussing a little and wasn't feeling too good. That leg was bleeding. It wasn't flopping, though, so I felt like the bone hadn't been busted. All in all it wasn't much of a wound. I've been gouged near as deep by a cactus thorn.

There was more than enough people around to do the doctoring, so I didn't make no effort to help out. I had already done a right smart more than I figured was my duty to a damn fool. I stood in front of the wagon and kept my eyes peeled on the Indians. I didn't figure they was likely to make a charge at the wagons, knowing how they was outmanned, but I also knowed that Indians would sometimes do the opposite of what you expected. It never hurt to be ready.

Well sir, first thing I knowed Samantha was there with a pan of water and a towel, and she was washing that feller's face and talking soft to him while Zeb and a couple of the men was pouring whiskey into the wound and holding him down. He used language that ought to never fall on a good woman's ears, but I suppose he wasn't thinking along them lines at the time. Pretty soon Zeb had the bleeding stopped and the wound tied up and was telling everybody the damage was nothing very serious. I could of told them that from the start. The feller had calmed down considerable. Samantha was still putting that wet cloth to his face and trying to make him feel better.

It didn't make *me* feel any better, I'll tell you.

Now that I had time and the inclination for a closer look, I could see that he was young, a good deal younger than me. He had several days' growth of whiskers, but there wasn't no tracks around the corners of his eyes yet. When he finally managed to tear his eyes away from Samantha he looked at me. He says, "You're the one that dragged me in here, ain't you?"

I already felt like that could of been a mistake, and

I didn't want to claim all the credit. I says, "One of them. Soledad Martinez was the other one."

He thanks us both and says, "That was sure a tight spot you-all got me out of."

I was about half mad, thinking how easy it would of been for some of us to have gotten ourselves killed. If it hadn't been for Zeb and Samantha, I'd of let him take his chances out there with them Indians.

I was about to walk off and leave him, but I decided to ask him, "What the hell was you doin' off out yonder by yourself, anyway? Didn't anybody ever tell you that Indians are dangerous?"

He says, "There's other things just as dangerous."

I seen the way Samantha was looking at him, with enough pity in her eyes to drown a gray mule, and I thought, *There sure is.* I walked out between the wagons and looked toward the mountains. The Indians was still out there, riding away but taking their time about it, kind of tempting the foolhardy to go chasing after them. There wasn't no fools with our wagons, though, unless you count that stranger.

When the Indians was clean gone I caught up my black and rode out to the stranger's horse. It was a little bay, still alive but too badly wounded to live. I pulled the saddle off of him, then put a bullet in his brain. I carried the saddle back to the wagon circle. A saddle ain't ever a cheap and easy thing to come by. I figured this stranger would need his to ride out of here as soon as he was able, which I hoped would be *real* soon.

Well sir, if you think you already begin to see the turn of things, you're plumb right. Just about the time I was beginning to have some dreams about buying me a ranch out west and settling down in a nest with Samantha, she gets a patient to worry about and mother-hen over. I've never understood it, but I've seldom seen it fail. Watch a nurse, and nine times out of ten she'll marry one of her patients. You can be as big as a mountain, stout as a bull, brave as a bear, rich as old Croesus, and chances are you won't get no more than a passing glance from a woman. But get yourself sick or hurt to where she can wait on you and play nurse to you, and you've got her in the palm of your hand.

I got to wishing it had been *me* with a wound in my leg. Then maybe I'd of got some attention. Way it was, I hardly even got a thank-you-sir.

There wasn't nothing to do but camp right where we was till we could tell about them Indians. We figured there was some risk they might go for some of their friends. If the subject was to be pursued any further, this was as good a place as any to do it. They had to come at us over a big open greasewood flat where they made a lot better target than we did.

Time I got all the necessaries took care of and went back to the Wentworth wagon, Samantha already knowed a great deal more about the stranger than I was interested in finding out. His name was Pete Ogden, she told me, and he had come from over around San Antonio someplace. He was on his way west to seek his fortune when he had run into the Indians, who had a little different plan worked out for him.

"You know something else?" she says. "He's a farmer."

Well, so had I been once, but I sure didn't brag about it.

She says, "If we try we might talk him into staying with us and locating in the same part of the country that we do."

I could tell by the way he kept looking at her that it wouldn't take any talking to convince him. It might take talking to keep him from it.

That old lady Addie was tickled to death over the way things turned out. She grinned at me like the jasper that's about to kick the stool out from under a man with the noose around his neck. I could've choked the old woman if there hadn't been so many witnesses.

Well sir, me and Soledad taken us a long ride early

the next morning, swinging over to them hills to look
for sign the Indians might be getting ready to come at
us again. The country was as clean as a hound's tooth.
We decided there wasn't anything to keep us from pro-
ceeding ahead except timidity.

Soledad was kind of the *caporal* over the Mexican
part of the wagon train. Seemed like a decent sort, a
man we could depend on. After that little set-to which
gained us a new passenger, he got to acting as an outrider. I'd scout out front. He'd trail along behind
the wagons, and far out toward the hills, making sure the
train didn't get sneaked up on from behind. About all
we ever seen out there was jackrabbits and *javalina*
hogs.

You'd be surprised how fast Pete Ogden's leg started
healing up. Of course he had him a good nurse that
seen after his welfare every spare minute she had; he
ought to've done good. Pretty soon he was getting
around on a cane, then limping about without it.
Looked to me like he was fit enough to start making
some real use of himself around the wagons. But Samantha said he oughtn't to rush nature.

Nature was rushing along pretty good, it seemed to
me. Nights, him and her would take out and walk
around the edge of the wagon circle, the way I'd tried
to do with her. Old Addie never would let us out of
her sight when it was *me*, but she didn't seem to worry
about Pete Ogden. Matter of fact, she would kind of
stick the knife in me and give it a twist every time she
seen the chance. She'd say, "Ain't they a handsome
couple?" or such as that.

I'd remember the old Bible story about how the Lord
handled all them sinners at the Tower of Babel by making them speak different languages so they couldn't
understand each other, and I'd wonder how come he
hadn't fixed it so men and women couldn't talk to one
another. It would of saved a lot of grief in this old

world, preacher. I'm surprised the Lord hasn't thought of it.

My eyes have always been pretty good. I could see by the look that came into Samantha's every time Pete Ogden passed in front of her that I could forget all them pretty little dreams I had been building up about her and me.

After awhile Pete got tired of riding in a wagon all day and volunteered to help out however he could. I mentioned the loose stock, thinking how it wouldn't hurt to let him eat dust at the tail end of the wagon train, bringing up the extra cattle and horses. He got the borrow of a horse and fell in back there and went to work. I watched him a right smart, and I'll have to admit he made a hand.

I was some disappointed about that. I had hoped he would show up as one of them slough-off types, and old Zeb would run him off from the train first time we came to a settlement. But he showed himself to be a willing worker and acted like he understood stock. There's nothing leaves a man as frustrated as wanting to dislike somebody and not finding anything solid to dislike him about.

It's even worse when you wind up owing him a debt. And one day pretty soon I found myself owing Pete Ogden.

We was way off out in that old dry country west of the Pecos River, where the Davis Mountains come down and cut across the desert, and you either have to climb over them or go way around or hunt a pass through. All the old wagon and stagecoach trails led through the passes, which is fine except when the Indians come looking for horses and hair. A nice narrow pass is just made to order for an Indian, like buffalo hump and eagle feathers. We came up to one, and there wasn't nothing else to do except me ride in there and see if there was anything waiting for us that we might not want to meet.

There was.

Did you ever accidentally strike a hornet's nest and watch them hornets pour out after you? I doubt that you did much watching because you was too busy running. That's the way it was with me. These stories you read about the Indian always knowing everything that goes on within a hundred miles of him are just so much imagination on the part of some Eastern writer that never heard an arrow sing by his left ear. I think I surprised them Apaches about as much as they surprised me, or I wouldn't of had a chance for any kind of head start.

I've known a few old men in my time that had a reputation as Indian fighters. They always told me that one secret of getting to be an *old* Indian fighter was to know when to run, and always ride a fast horse just in case you come to one of them times unexpected. I was riding that Santos black and doing real good. I could see the wagons going into a circle ahead of me. Way out behind, Soledad was spurring like hell to catch up to the train.

I was making a dandy gain on them Indians. I was maybe three hundred yards from the train and at least a couple of hundred ahead of them Apaches when I seen somebody come spurring out to meet me from the wagons, firing a pistol as he came. Now, talk about useless . . . somebody shooting a pistol at Indians five hundred yards away is just plain wasteful.

Another old story you hear sometimes is that Indians couldn't shoot a gun straight. That's about as truthful as a lot of the other Indian yarns. I was looking back over my shoulder and seen one of those Indians stop his horse, jump off, drop to one knee and fire. I seen the smoke, and a second or two later that horse of mine turned a flip.

I hit the ground like some giant had picked me up and throwed me as hard as he could. All the breath was knocked out of me, and that horse's rump came down and pounded on both of my legs. I reckon it was imagination, but I thought I could already hear them Indians singing over my hair. I tried to get up and run, but I didn't have the breath in me, and my legs was both too numb. I sort of halfway pushed myself to my feet. My eyes was so blurry I couldn't see which was the way to the wagon train, and which to the Indians.

I heard a horse come running at me, and tried to shoot my pistol at it, but it was all jammed with dirt and wouldn't fire. I throwed my hands up to try and protect my head, because I figured I was about to get a stone ax right over my ear.

Somebody hollered. "Grab on! Let's get out of here!"

It was Pete Ogden. He leaned over and reached out his arm, and all of a sudden my legs didn't hurt me a bit. I grabbed onto him. He socked the spurs to that horse and held me as tight as he could up against the saddle. My legs was both hanging off on one side, dragging through the low brush. I could hear them Indians hollering behind us. I could hear that horse straining with the double load, and I could hear Pete Ogden promising him all kinds of good things if he wouldn't let the Indians catch us.

You never tried to hang onto a running horse when all the breath's been knocked out of you, I suppose. Under any ordinary circumstances it would be hard to do. But knowing what was back there to catch me if I fell off, I didn't have much trouble at it.

I heard the wagon people shooting, trying to drive the Indians back, but I couldn't see anything. The saddlehorn kept punching me in the ribs and knocking the breath back out of me every time I could get a little air in. We made it to the wagons. Pete Ogden jumped his horse over a wagontongue and dropped me on the ground like I was a sack of oats. I was still in a daze when people picked me up and started hunting over me for wounds. By the time I could get enough breath back to tell them I was all right, there wasn't a secret birth-mark about my body that half the wagon train didn't know. My clothes was pretty well torn off of me, first by the fall when my horse went down, and then by the brush Pete drug me through.

Directly I was laying under the shade of a wagon and looking up at Pete Ogden the same way he had looked at me the time before. Except that I didn't have any wounds for Samantha to fuss over, and get her all moon-eyed.

Saying "thank you" never was hard for me like it is for some people, but this time it was like pulling my own teeth out to get it said. I almost gagged over it. I finally told Pete I was right obliged to him for his little favor, and what the hell was he shooting up all that ammunition for? He said he was hoping he might scare the Indians away, which showed how little he knowed about Indians. I hoped he knowed more about farming.

You might think what Pete done just squared up a debt he owed me, but I knowed deep inside that it was more. The only reason I had gone out to rescue him was because Samantha shamed me into it, and I knowed the others was going out anyway. But Pete Ogden came after me all by himself, and without any-body shaming him. This young farmer was a *man*, and I resented him for it!

Talk about things turning out backwards . . . this time it was *me* that was laid up and needing help, and all Samantha could do was hug Pete Ogden's neck and tell him how brave he was, how scared she was that something might of happened to him. Nary a word about what might of happened to me.

A man who tells it around that he understands women is just letting everybody know how big a fool he really is.

I got my breath back awhile later. Zeb asked me what I thought we ought to do about getting through that pass. I told him it seemed to me that if them Indians wanted it so much, the neighborly thing was to let them have it and work on north. Maybe we could find us another one that wasn't being used. Soledad rode out and got my saddle back for me when the Indians was gone, the way I had done for Pete Ogden. The Indians had carried off my carbine. I sure hated to leave that black horse. He was as fast a one as ever I rode, excepting maybe my Tennessee gray. But they don't make horses that can outrun a bullet.

That was the last of the Indian trouble for us, though Pete Ogden didn't take Samantha outside the wagon circle for any more night walking. They just stayed at the wagon and spooned in front of everybody. Odd thing happened, too. Pete Ogden had always seemed grateful to me for helping drag him away from the Indians, and after he done the same thing for me he got downright friendly, like we was old partners or something. I didn't encourage him. Even if he didn't know it, I owed him a right smart more than he owed me, and owing a man a debt don't endear him to you.

It got to be common knowledge amongst the wagon folks that when they got to El Paso him and Samantha was going to hunt up a preacher. There wasn't nobody prouder over it than Addie Wentworth. She had finally got to where she would even treat me like a white man, knowing I wasn't no danger to her niece any longer.

But I could tell something was bothering Pete. I'd catch him sometimes watching her when she wasn't looking, and there was a worry in his eyes that got to worrying *me* a little. I got to suspicioning that maybe he already had him a wife back wherever he came from, and things had gone so far that he was afraid to tell anybody. I got to thinking maybe there was hope for me yet.

One night Pete tapped me on the arm and gave me a nod of his head. He motioned for me to walk out with him a ways, past the wagons. By this time we had got amongst some Mexican settlements along the Rio

Grande, and we wasn't much concerned about Indians anymore. It wasn't far to El Paso.

Pete says to me, "Joe, I got something to tell you. If I don't do it now, I'm going to bust."

I figured he was going to confess to me about the wife he had went off and left behind him. I was going to hear him out and then do the manly thing: knock him halfway to El Paso.

He says, "You figured me for a stranger when I joined this train, but I wasn't, not quite. You never seen *me* before, but I seen *you*, Joe. I knowed who you was from the start."

That throwed me a little. I just looked at him and tried to think back to when I could of ever crossed his trail before. I was afraid he knowed I was Joe Peeler instead of Joe Pepper.

He says, "I rode into Catclaw one night, and I spotted you with your badge on. I made it a point to stay out of your sight. I needed me a stake to go on west; I was flat busted. I waited till you was out of town, and I taken it."

He didn't have to tell me any more. I guessed the rest of it. I says, "You're the bank robber I hunted all over hell and half of Texas for."

He just nodded at me. He says, "I was hungry, and it seemed like a smart thing to do. Now that I've throwed in with these good folks, and you and Samantha, I'm ashamed of myself. I can see that I really ain't good enough for her. I ain't worth much, Joe."

That wasn't exactly the truth. He was worth five hundred dollars to me, right there the way he stood. That is, when I delivered him in at El Paso and notified the bank at Catclaw.

I was a little put out at him. I says, "Have you got an idea how many miles I rode hunting for you? I wore saddle-blisters on my butt and went hungry so much that I had to punch a new hole in my belt."

He tells me, "I'm sorry, Joe. I didn't know you at

the time, and I thought it would be funny to have people hunting for me and not finding me. It was the first time in my life anybody paid any real attention to me."

"If they'd of caught you they'd of paid you more attention than you really wanted."

Pete says, "I still got nearly all the money, Joe. I just spent a little dab in Mexico, is all. I'd like to get you to send it back to them for me." He reached inside his shirt and brought out a little canvas pouch. I ran my hands into it. I could tell it wasn't no big lot of money.

He says, "There's a shade over nine hundred dollars. I never spent more than twenty-thirty of it."

I thought about my little leather bag of gold. I wasn't in the pouch. I says, "There's something else, Pete. You got something that belongs to me personal."

He didn't act like he understood, so I told him. He just blinked at me. He says, "I didn't see nothing like that. All I taken was the currency."

Something about the way he looked at me, I knowed he was telling me the truth. Which meant that somebody else had lied to me.

Clopton! Old man Dietert's number-one helper had been the one who opened the safe for Pete, and the one who shut it afterwards. *That* crooked coyote had got off with my gold and blamed it on Pete Ogden.

I cussed a blue streak. Pete thought it was against him. He says kind of sorrowful, "I don't blame you for being mad at me. I got it coming. You want to turn me in to the law at El Paso, I'll stand ready to take my medicine."

There it was, the opportunity to get Pete Ogden out of the way, to maybe have a new chance at Samantha. To rub old lady Addie's nose in the truth. The chance I'd been waiting for, and I spoiled it.

I got to feeling noble and generous, which is a feeling I never had but a few times, and generally always lived to regret. I says to Pete, "You really love that girl? You really mean to try and make her happy the rest of her life?"

"I would if I could. But she won't want me when she finds out what I am. I ain't worthy of her."

"She don't have to know about it. I'll turn in the money for you. I'll send a letter back to Catclaw and tell them I found you and had to kill you. As far as they'll be concerned you're dead and buried, and the case is closed. Nobody ever has to know except me and you."

I don't reckon Pete had expected that. I do believe he was about to break down and cry. He says, "I'll owe you for the rest of my life, Joe."

Better *him* owing *me* than the other way around. What he didn't know wouldn't hurt him. I wasn't really all that noble. I knowed if I was to turn Pete in to the law, Samantha would blame me more than she blamed him. Chances was she wouldn't of spoken to me again, ever. All I would've got out of it would've been the reward. I figured to get the reward anyway.

Well sir, we got in to El Paso, and they had theirselves a wedding, and Pete Ogden moved right into Samantha's wagon. Old lady Addie grinned at me, so much as to say she was glad Samantha had got herself an honest, hardworking young farmer boy instead of a crooked, whiskey-drinking, gambling gunfighter. And I grinned back at her because I knowed a lot more about it than she did.

The wagon train pulled out for the valley where the farmers figured to sink their plows into new ground. I stayed in El Paso because it would of hurt too much to see Samantha and Pete Ogden together.

I really did intend to turn that money in at first. Then I got to thinking. They owed me a five-hundred-dollar reward for finding the bank robber in the first place. On top of that, they owed me for that bag of gold Clopton had got away with. I figured the money Pete had given me didn't quite cover all I had coming to me. But I was still in a generous mood and willing to accept my loss. I just kept what I had.

I did write old man Dietert a letter, though. Best I remember, I told him something like this:

Deer Mr Dietert,

Just a line to let you know I come across that bank robber and we had a fight and I am sorry to relate that I was obliged to kill him. Before he died he told me he had went and spent all the money so there aint none to send to you. I saved his ear to mail you as proof but it spoiled on me and I dont think you want it. He also told me he didnt get as much as was supposed to have been lost and that he suspected somebody in the bank must have helped himself and blamed him for it. I was thinkin maybe it might be smart if you and Sheriff Smathers was to surprise Clopton with a serch of his house, you might be surprised at what you come up with. He always looked kind of shifty eyed to me.
Best regards and yours truely.

Joe Pepper

I would of liked to have been there if they found my gold sack on him. I never did hear one way or the other, but years later I run across somebody from Cat-claw and asked if they knowed old man Dietert or his helper Clopton. They said the old man had finally died of a heart seizure, and Clopton had long ago run off to Mexico. Seemed there was trouble of some kind, and he got away with nothing much more than his britches.

Chapter 6

I'm ashamed to tell you, preacher, but for a little while I tried to drown my sorrows in bad whiskey and sinful surroundings. Old El Paso was a good place for a man who wanted to do that kind of a thing. They had people there who was experts at helping you. I consorted with women of bad character and men who was worse. Pretty soon that fat money belt had shrunk to a little of nothing. One morning I come face to face with myself at the mirror and done some pretty stern talking. I had to get myself into some productive kind of labor.

So I went back to gambling. I know you don't approve of it, but the way I done it, there wasn't a lot of gamble in it. I cheated. Not all the time, mind you; just when I had to. Nine out of ten of them people didn't have to be cheated; they would just naturally beat themselves. Pretty soon I had built me up a first-rate stake again. Not as much as I had come to town with, but enough to set me up in a game where I stood a chance to come away with some real important money.

I had given up on my dream of a home with Samantha, of course, but the idea of another ranch hadn't altogether left me yet. I had a notion that if I could clean up good in El Paso I'd drift on out to Arizona and maybe buy me a ranch and live the rest of my life in peace.

At one place in town they had a high-stakes game in a back room almost every night. Big cow men and big mine people would come there and try their hand against the best gamblers in town. Their luck wasn't usually any too good, but they would keep coming back, most of them, hoping the next time Lady Luck would turn her face on them instead of her back. That's what kept them high-stakes games going, was the hope that when a man lost big, he might go back and win big. Now and again one would, just enough to keep the others hoping. Meanwhile them gamblers skimmed the cream off of a lot of the cow business and the mining without ever getting cow manure on their boots or picking up a shovel.

The place was a saloon known as the Rio Bravo, which was the name a lot of the Mexicans had for the Rio Grande. Owner was a man named Frank Feller. He was a fair-to-middling poker player and sometimes sat in on the games, but mostly he was a shill for the real gambler of the outfit, a tall, spidery kind of a gent named Arthur Phelps. Folks around town called him "Slick" Phelps, but not to his face. He was said to be a good shot. He had long hands that had never known a callus, and tapering fingers that could make a deck of cards do almost anything except sing a hymn. Feller provided the place and bankrolled Phelps's games and got a percentage of the take, though they always pretended the game was Phelps's own, and Feller appeared to lose a right smart to him. That was just to bring the suckers in.

I had got a little rusty at the game, since them people in Catclaw hadn't been much of a challenge, but I polished it up in El Paso and bided my time till I thought I was ready to match up with Slick Phelps. Finally, after I had been there two months, I sat in on the game one night, figuring I was ready. Now, I considered myself a right smooth hand, but I could tell right off that I wasn't a match for Phelps. I lost a thousand dollars in one night and knowed he was cheating me more than I was cheating him, but I never once caught him at it.

So I went back to lower-stakes games in other places to practice up some more. I practiced cheating other people, then I would turn around and cheat myself on purpose so they wouldn't catch on to what I was doing. I wasn't after these small fry anyway, except for the practice they gave me. I had my sights set on cleaning out Slick Phelps. Finally I went back and sat in with him again. I thought I had improved to where I could give him a contest. It didn't take me but two hours and another thousand dollars to figure out I wasn't good enough to wipe the dust off of his boots.

I noticed a couple of things about Slick Phelps. One thing, he never drank. The only thing he ever taken was a cup of coffee, which seemed to sharpen him up. Whiskey was for idiots when it came to high-stakes gambling. It just slowed the hands and dulled the eyes. Then Slick Phelps would come down his web and grab you like a fly. Another thing he always done was to excuse himself every couple of hours. He would walk outside and take a little air, and he would ease his kidneys. Little as you might think about it, the strain on a man's kidneys in a long game can be just the edge that a smoother player needs on him. Slick Phelps didn't give nobody any edge.

When Phelps was out, Feller would take over the game. He was no cowboy playing for matches on a saddle blanket, of course, but he wasn't a pimple on Phelps's backside when it come to the pinch. Often as not he would lose more than he taken in, and when Phelps came back it was up to him to recover the house losses. Some of them high-stakes players always kind of waited for Phelps to take his constitutional, then they would bet big against Feller, trying to get back what they could.

I knowed if I stayed in El Paso till I had a beard to my belly, I would never beat Slick Phelps. Not in any ordinary way, that is. But Joe Pepper didn't get his reputation doing everything the ordinary way.

They had an outhouse behind the saloon, up against the alley. I set myself out there one night in the shadows across the other side and watched Phelps. He done everything by habit. He would come out the back door and stand on the stoop two or three minutes, looking up at the stars. I figured he was probably looking for sign of rain, which was a waste of time at El Paso. Next thing he would do was to roll himself a cigarette and stand there and smoke it about half up. He never smoked inside, at the game. Cigarettes was a distraction, and he didn't allow himself no distractions.

Finally he would throw the cigarette away, walk to the outhouse, take care of nature's call, then stop at the washstand, wash and dry his hands, and go back in to the game. I watched him all that night, and never once did he vary from the routine.

I had sort of worked up an idea in my head. The sheriff was an agreeable sort of feller, considering the things he had to put up with, and he generally rode around town in a buggy. One night there was a disturbance in one of the fancy houses down toward the river, and he went trotting his horses down there to see about it. I trailed along behind him in the dark. While he was inside I fished in the back of that buggy and found a set of handcuffs. I didn't steal them, exactly, I just took the borrow of them awhile. I didn't have a key to them, but I kept pestering them a couple of days, off and on, till I learned how to open them up with a piece of wire.

The night I brought off my plan, I taken all the

money I had been able to work up and shoved it into
my shirt. I taken the handcuffs and a fair piece of rawhide rope, and I set myself up in the dark behind the
Rio Bravo. I let Slick Phelps go the first time he came
out. The second time I watched him smoke his cigarette, and watched him go to the house out back. When
he went to the washstand and poured a pan of water
out of the bucket, I stepped up behind him and gave
him what people used to call a cowpuncher shampoo.
That is, I fetched him a lick up beside the head with
the barrel of my six-shooter. You never seen a tall man
fold up so limber.

I had found where there was an old empty corral a
piece off down the street. I drug him down there in the
dark while he was still enjoying the benefit of the
shampoo. I laid him on the ground, handcuffed him to
the bottom of the fencepost and tied his feet with the
rawhide rope. I stuffed a handkerchief into his mouth
and tied another one around it to where he couldn't
holler. Time he come to he was trussed up like a hog
on a spit.

I dusted myself off, walked in the front door of the
Rio Bravo and marched back to that high-stakes game
in the rear room. I bought me a stack of chips and set
in to see how much I could win from Frank Feller.

He didn't seem bothered right at first when I started
beating him. He would glance over towards the door
once in a while, figuring Phelps would walk in any
minute and polish me off in short order. My stack of
chips started growing right peart. Before long Feller
was spending a lot of time looking at that door. Every
time he did I taken the occasion to improve my hand
a little. Sweat started running down into his eyes, and
he would rub a sleeve over them, and I would see him
pull a new card out of that sleeve. That didn't bother
me much; as long as I could see what he was doing, I
could do him one better.

He got to talking about how something must of happened to Phelps, and maybe we ought to wait up the game for him. I told him it didn't matter to me whether Phelps was in the game or not, that if Feller was able to play for the house there wasn't no reason why the game shouldn't go on. One by one the other players dropped out. By and by Feller had dropped so much money to me that he couldn't afford to quit. He kept thinking, I guess, that Phelps would finally show up and bail him out of trouble.

But Phelps didn't show up. I had picked me a good place to put him, where nobody was apt to come across him till daylight. By daylight I figured to have myself that ranch in Arizona.

What I *did* get was something different. By the time the sun came up and hit Feller in the eyes through the glass panes of the east window, he didn't own that window anymore. *I* did. The Rio Bravo was mine.

The story told around town was that somebody figured Phelps would have money in his pockets when he stepped outside that night. They waylaid him to rob him, then handcuffed him to give theirselves plenty of time to get away. Most people agreed it was probably Mexicans from over in Paso del Norte, across the river. It was the custom if you couldn't find out who had done something to just blame it on the Mexicans.

Most people accepted that theory, but Frank Feller never did. I think he had it figured out from the time they found Phelps where I had left him. He came to me at the Rio Bravo, where I was figuring what color I wanted to paint the front. He was loud and threatening; most people hadn't heard much about Joe Pepper at the time. He left there in a lot worse shape than he came, one eye shut and the other hard to see out of. He went then to Slick Phelps and convinced him it was me who had done him to a turn.

I wished he hadn't done that, because I figured on making Phelps a proposition to stay on and play for me the same way he had played for Feller. That loud-mouth ruined it.

Phelps sent word he was coming to have satisfaction. I sent him back a note telling him I was already sat-isfied and didn't want no trouble. People around the saloon told me he was a man to watch out for; he had helped several undertakers across the country to get on their feet and pay their bills. I decided if that was the way it had to be, I didn't want anybody saying I wasn't ready.

I taken me a rifle and walked across the street to a little barbershop. I sat down where I could watch the front of the place through the window while the barber cut my hair. By and by Slick Phelps came walking down the street on them long, spindly legs. Just before he got there he shucked his swallowtail coat and laid it across a hitching rack where it wouldn't get dirty and wouldn't be in his way. He had a six-shooter on his hip.

Up to then I had entertained some notion I might still be able to talk to him. After seeing him I decided that talk was the last thing he had come for. He stopped in front of the Rio Bravo. He hollers in, "Pepper, you coming out here?" He drawed his pistol and held it.

Them fellers that drawed before they faced you was hard to beat.

I didn't say anything. I taken the barber's cloth from around my neck and got up from the chair.

Phelps waited a minute and hollered again. Then he walked inside. I reckon he didn't find me in there, be-cause in a minute or two he was back. Meantime I had stepped down into the street, into the sunshine. It just so happened that this was late in the afternoon, and my saloon faced west toward the sun. Afterwards, some people accused me of working it all out this way. I never did admit to that.

He had been inside long enough that his eyes was accustomed to the dark instead of the light. I says,

"Slick, how about me and you working out a deal? We'd make good partners."

He hadn't come there to talk business. He raised up his pistol, but the afternoon sun hit him in the eyes. I leveled my rifle and taken a good clean sight while he started to shoot wild. You can imagine, preacher, it wasn't no contest.

I sure did wish I hadn't had to shoot Phelps. Him and me could of made us a right smart of money together if he hadn't listened to Frank Feller so much. If I had had my choices I would rather of laid out Frank Feller.

Well sir, that's how come Joe Pepper to start making a reputation in and around El Paso. Folks figured I must be something special to have beaten Slick Phelps, but I didn't take no credit and still don't. I'd still rather bring a man around to my persuasion than to kill him.

Them days they had a custom in El Paso. Somebody had nailed a big board to a tree in the middle of town, and it was kind of a bulletin board for everybody to see and use. Somebody had something he wanted to sell, he tacked a note on the board. Somebody wanted to call a man a thief or a liar in public, he wrote it out and tacked it up on the board. A friend told me there was a note on the board that I ought to go see. Frank Feller had wrote it. He called me twelve kinds of a cheat and a black-hearted killer. I looked all over town for him. I had it in mind to take him over to the board and persuade him to eat that note, with witnesses. But folks told me he had remembered some business in Mexico.

That Rio Bravo turned out to be quite a place. I'd never had me a saloon and gambling house before. Pretty soon I gave up any notions I'd had about a ranch. The cow business never was half what people sometimes made it out to be. A man can starve himself into a little bitty shadow trying to nurse along a bunch of money-losing cows. A man who has a good saloon is always popular, especially in a thirsty place like El Paso was. Any direction you came from, when you got to El Paso you was dry to the bone.

I taken over the run of the games. I handpicked me a couple of good house gamblers, bankrolled them and taken a split of the proceeds. Once in a while one of them would get to putting aside too much money for himself and start to feeling independent, and then I'd have to get into a game with him myself and teach him a little humility, and also take enough money from him that he appreciated working for me again.

There's an art to handling employees. Some people never learn it.

Things was running my way for a change. I won't try to tell you we run a hundred-percent honest house because you wouldn't believe me, and I don't see no point in telling a lie if there's no profit in it. But I will say we tried to give everybody as even a shake as they could get anywhere in town, and better than most. We had the odds with the house anyway because I didn't keep men around working for me that wasn't almost as good a hand with the pasteboards as I was. And we tried never to clean a man out of his last dime; we always quit in time to leave him a taw. That way maybe he would come back for another game. Take a man's taw away from him and you've lost a customer for good.

About the only worry I had was politics. I never seen a town so mean on politics as El Paso was. The Democrats and the Republicans was at each other's throats. And there was factions within both of them groups that was fighting each other almost as hard as they fought the opposite party. Me being an old Confederate veteran naturally leaned me a little toward the Democrats, but I tried never to worry about a man's politics when I played him. I taken money gladly from Democrat and Republican alike.

It was during that time that I first run onto Burney

Northcutt. Folks told me he was a big rancher from west of the Pecos. He wasn't an old man then, the way *you've* knowed him in late years. He was just sloping over the hill into middle age. He had a pinch of gray in his hair and a dab in his mustache, but his eyes was pure fire. He had built a big spread by having the guts to take what he wanted and the iron will to hang onto it. He had fought Yankees and Apaches and bandits and drouth. He had a natural taste for combat; it was like fresh air and sunshine to him. When things ran quiet for too long he would take an itchy notion to come into El Paso, ream out his innards with strong whiskey, and see if his luck at the tables was as good as his luck on the range.

It never was. Folks told me he had always lost to Slick Phelps. Nothing changed when I taken over the Rio Bravo. He lost to me every time we ever played.

He would cuss like a muleskinner and threaten to shoot me, but as long as he kept his hand away from his pistol I didn't pay him much mind. I wasn't one of them people who rankled at every insult and called on a man to apologize or draw his gun, not if I knowed he still had some gambling money left in his pockets. Anger is bad for the digestion, and none too good for business, either.

Half a dozen times I could of shot Burney Northcutt, and not six people in El Paso would of criticized me for it. Maybe if I'd done it then, I wouldn't be in the fix you find me in here tonight.

But of course that's spilt milk, and there's no use rolling in it.

I found me a nice-looking girl down on the row. She had corn-silk hair and big blue eyes that seemed to touch a chord in me someway. I taken her out of circulation and kept her in my own private stock, so to speak. I got to where I didn't waste much time fretting over Samantha. She was just another game I had played and lost. If a man's going to be any kind of a gambler, he's got to get so he don't cry over his losses.

I had me some good times there in El Paso. Things rocked along pretty smooth for a long spell. That's not to say there wasn't little difficulties once in a while over a game, and once I had to kill a holdup man who tried to bulldoze the place and take all the money. But I went for a whole year once without ever having to draw a gun on anybody. Joe Pepper's reputation went a long ways toward holding down trouble.

One day that girl of mine told me she heard a rumor that Frank Feller had been seen in town. He was talking about getting even, some of the girls had said. I had got kind of careless in my good fortune, but I taken to sitting with my back to the wall and watching the doors and windows. I didn't figure him for a face-out shooter, not after what happened to Slick Phelps.

After a while I decided the reports must of been false, because I never did see or hear anything of him. Then all of a sudden I had something a lot more than Frank Feller to worry about. A new face showed up in the high-stakes games.

This feller didn't look a bit like Slick Phelps or I'd of taken him for his brother. He had Phelps's same techniques with the cards. He had the same kind of long, tapering fingers, the same quick and easy shuffle that left you convinced you had missed seeing something but never could tell exactly what. And every time he sat down at the table, the stack of chips in front of him growed while everybody else's got smaller and smaller. The gamblers that worked with me played him first, till he cleaned them out. I gave them a good talking-to about paying attention to business, but that didn't do no good. They was simply outclassed. So finally I sat in on the game with him myself.

It would of been better if the doctor and sheriff had come along and quarantined the place for smallpox. He taken me the way Grant taken Richmond. He got me in the same shape that I had got Frank Feller, in so deep that I couldn't afford to keep on but couldn't afford to quit, either. When it was all over, he had the Rio Bravo, and I had had me *some* experience. He left me with a hundred dollars—said he never liked to leave a man without a taw.

That's when I first seen the fine hand of Frank Feller at work. He showed up looking like a cat that's stole the cream and left the family nothing but the skim milk. He announced to all and sundry that he had gone all the way to California hunting a gambler good enough to take me to the poorhouse.

For a little while I studied on killing him, and I expect I would of done it if I could of decided on a way. No way I could think of seemed like it was quite bloody enough. Then after awhile I began to see that he hadn't done nothing more to me than I had done to him. The more I thought about it, the more it got to looking funny, except I couldn't get myself to laugh much.

Sooner or later, I figured, somebody else would take him. He wouldn't die rich. I would live to see him flat on his butt again.

But while I was waiting for that, I couldn't just sit around. I had got in the habit of eating regular. That hundred dollars wouldn't take me far. In fact, I sat in on a low-ante poker game and lost most of it in about the same time as I would of spent eating a good meal.

Lady Luck had turned her back on me. I don't know what I done to sour the old girl on me, but whatever it was, it must of been something big. Got to where I couldn't hardly beat a bunch of cowboys playing on a saddleblanket.

My girl with the corn-silk hair was spending her nights with other people. I was eating *chili* and sleeping on a bedroll down by the river when somebody came to me with a story that Don Luis Terrazas was hiring guards on the big ranch he was building down in Chihuahua. He was paying good money to *gringo pisto-*

leros. I borrowed a few dollars from some friends and bought me a few days' supplies and struck off across that sandy desert south of El Paso.

I didn't have no trouble getting the job. My only trouble was getting to like it. I never did. Terrazas had been a soldier under Juarez, people told me, and he grabbed up a big chunk of Chihuahua state after they run the Frenchmen out. I reckon that was his reward. Naturally there were already some natives there who didn't want to give up what they figured was theirs. He needed people who could use a gun and convince them they was wrong.

It was some of the easiest money I ever made, away from a gaming table, but the job always had a sour taste to it. Every time I brought back a runaway *peon* on a rope, or somebody they had classed as a *bandido*, I'd get a whiff of the cells they throwed them in, and I'd remember the one Captain Santos had used for me. They all had the same smell to them. It's a stench that, once it gets in your nostrils, it never quite leaves you the rest of your life. It marks you someway, like the smallpox.

I got sick of it. So one night I drawed my pay and slipped down to the cells. I gave the two guards there a cowpuncher shampoo. Then I taken the keys and opened all the doors I could get to and let the prisoners out. Some of them taken to running the way I expected them to. Others just sat there, afraid to try to get away. They had been *peons* all their lives to one *patrón* or another, and the idea of freedom was beyond their thinking. I didn't have time to stay around and give them any Fourth of July lecture. I figured Don Luis would probably have some of his gunfighters on my tail by daylight, and it was a long ways from the mountains of Chihuahua back up to the Rio Grande. I taken my horse, and a couple of Don Luis's that seemed like they wanted to follow me. When I looked behind me after sunup, I didn't see nothing back there but desert.

I tried the cards again in El Paso, but Lady Luck still had me on the list. I had to sell the Terrazas horses to be able to eat. I thought about going back to the kind of work I done at Catclaw, but the sheriff wasn't hiring. He didn't care much for retired gambling-house owners, or for men that had carried a pistol for Terrazas. Kind of a narrow-minded sort, he was.

I thought maybe I'd go bring in fugitives for the reward, but that turned out not to be worth all the wear and tear, either. I guess it taken an awful crime out in that part of the country to make them offer much of a reward, they was used to so much devilment anyway. Most people who had the law after them would run off down into Mexico, and I couldn't afford to cross the river. Don Luis and his *pistoleros* had a long memory for faces.

Like I've said before, one thing I always had was the sense to know when the gravy was going thin, and it was time to change. It was bully for me that I'd built up a right smart reputation. The word had passed around the country that Joe Pepper was a good hand with a gun. An outfit over in New Mexico was mining silver, and they had been having trouble getting their stuff out. A bunch of bold and brassy *hombres* kept riding in and taking it away from them. The law wasn't doing them much good, seemed like. Everybody knowed to their own satisfaction who was taking the silver, but they didn't have proof. Without proof the law couldn't do much—or wouldn't—so the mine owners came and asked if I could help them. I told them if they paid enough, there wasn't no practical limit to what I could do.

They was, I thought, kind of generous.

One thing people always use around a mining camp is dynamite. I taken me a bundle of it, rode back up into the mountains where the robbers stayed, and located their cabin. There wasn't much to it; they didn't expect no trouble with the law, and they didn't hardly even have a guard out. All I had to do was to tap the one lone sentry over the head kind of businesslike. The rest of them was inside, playing poker with the take from the last robbery. I planted that dynamite up beside the house, lit the fuse and moved out a little ways to watch.

You never seen a poker game break up quite as sudden. That cabin was poorly built anyhow. When the smoke cleared I only seen two of them come out of it, and I picked them off with my rifle.

After that the boys over in that district sort of lost interest in stealing other people's silver shipments. The local law was a little put out about it and said I had denied them boys the protection of a trial by jury. But the mine owners was happy, and they was the ones that paid me, so I just made a couple of suggestions to the local law, none of which they took.

I stayed on the payroll a good while, till the mine owners was sure their trouble was over. They knowed some people having similar difficulties up in the northern part of the state and sent me up there with a letter of recommendation. I was hired on the spot and told that anything I wanted to do, they would back me up. "Due process of law" in that country just meant that every man taken care of himself. After I had laid out three of them boys on a board, the rest decided the high altitude wasn't good for their health, and they moved out to a warmer climate.

There again I came in for a certain amount of slander. There was some folks who said I didn't give them boys a sporting chance, but I did. I sent them word before I came that they'd be a right smart healthier if they left the country before I got there. They didn't take my advice.

One thing, preacher, there never has been one of my bullets ever found in a man's back, except a couple of times when they was trying to run away to escape arrest. I always got a man from the front side, even if that exposed me to a little danger myself.

Naturally I had work in that part of the country as long as any of the wild bunch was still around. I done pretty good for some years, drifting from one mining section to another across New Mexico and Arizona, and for a time clear over into California. There was times when I didn't have to do anything except show up. The sticky-fingered crowd would hear Joe Pepper was in the vicinity, and they would just naturally go hunting for a different place to ply their trade. Couple of times the mining people decided I hadn't done anything to earn the money they promised me, and I had to use some persuasion to bring them around to my way of thinking. Last I knowed, there was still a "wanted" flyer out for me in California, charging me with robbery. But it wasn't me that done the robbery, it was *them*. They backed off from what they duly owed me, and I had to collect the bill the best way I could. I tell you, preacher, I found out a long time ago that all the people who go to rob you don't do it with a gun. There's some big-business men that needed planting about as much as the people they sent me after.

I read in one of them penny-dreadfuls where I was supposed to have been in the Lincoln County war, and ridden with Billy the Kid and such as that. A lie, every word of it. I had no part in that war atall.

Truth of the matter is, I figured there was money to be made out of that Lincoln County mess and went over there to see if I could hire on. Either side, it didn't matter. Way I figured it, both sides was a little shady, but their money would spend good.

It was a wasted trip. Each side figured I was a spy for the other, and I was damn lucky to escape from there with my life.

I never stayed in one place long enough to ever get elected as a sheriff. Once in a while a sheriff would hire me for a deputy, but seemed like there was always

somebody against me. They would hear or read some
wild story like them lies in the newspapers and the
penny-dreadfuls, and some righteous citizen would
raise up in indignation and want me run out of the
country. Times, it got awful hard to make an honest
dollar.

Such as that would occasionally lead me to have to
take jobs that I would as soon of left alone. Like that
Johnson County war in Wyoming. Now, *there* was a
fiasco. You've probably heard of it.

There was a bunch of big cattlemen up yonder that
claimed a considerable part of Wyoming as their range.
And there was a bunch of homesteaders and nesters
and little cattle raisers and so forth that sort of figured
they also had a right to some of the land. A thing like
that naturally leads to a certain amount of unpleasantness. It also leads to jobs for people like me.

I was sure needing work at the time. I'd been back
in El Paso, finding out to my own dissatisfaction that
Lady Luck still hadn't eased up on me for whatever it
was I done that offended her. Every once in a while I
would hope to catch her looking the other way, and I'd
sit in on a high-stakes poker game. But she always
looked around and seen me before my stack of chips
got too high.

I had a visit from an old friend who had put me onto
a job or two before. If I would take the train to Paris,
over in East Texas, he said, and meet a man there by
the name of Tom Smith, I was a cinch for work. The
pay was to be good. I just barely had me enough money
left for a train ticket and a few days' eating, so I went.
This Smith had rounded up a bunch of other people,
same as me, all of them supposed to be men of nerve
and good with a gun. He didn't tell us what we was to
do except that we was supposed to serve warrants on
some bad characters and to draw five dollars a day and
expenses. On top of that we would get a bonus of fifty
dollars for any man we had to kill. Them days, five

dollars wasn't bad, especially when your axle was dragging on the ground.

He told us to be quiet and say nothing to anybody. We went up to Denver and then on to Cheyenne with a cattleman named Wolcott. He was one of them that had decided to hire us for the job. I taken a disliking to him right off, because I could tell he didn't like *us*. He let us know that we wasn't nothing but hired gunfighters, and not in the class with the "gentlemen" who was paying us to take care of the work they was too clean-handed to do by themselves. He was an old man by then, which I reckon lots of people would of said *I* was, too. He had been an officer for the Union during the Civil War. That might of been another reason I couldn't take to him much. There had been a whole new generation growed up since that war; they had never smelled powder. I think maybe they put too much faith in him because he *had*. The truth is, he was probably too old to lead an expedition like ours.

They fixed us up with horses and ammunition in Cheyenne, and we pulled out for Casper on a special train with all the blinds down so people wouldn't notice us. We got to Casper in the cold dark of the morning, caught our horses from the stock car and headed out so we wouldn't be seen by the townspeople after the sun came up. The whole thing was a bad go, right from the start. A bunch of the horses got away. It had been raining, so the wagons kept sticking in the mud, and it was cold enough to bite a Texas man to the bone, especially if he was running to gray hair the way I was.

It wasn't till about this time that they ever really told us just what we was expected to do. Seemed like the cattlemen had been having lots of trouble with thieves. What we was supposed to do was make a roundup of these thieves and arrest them. If they resisted arrest we was supposed to shoot them. Seemed like the cattlemen hoped they would *all* resist arrest. It would of been a lot simpler that way.

You've probably read since that a lot of the men they was after wasn't really thieves at all, but just people who was resisting them and laying claim to lands that the cattlemen had been using. We didn't know nothing about that at the time. Way I looked at it, I was working for the man who paid me. If he said a man was a thief, that man was a thief. If I thought different, I asked for the wages I had already earned, and I rode off.

I'd never been to Wyoming in my life. I had no reason to think these cattlemen might be lying to us. For five dollars a day, which I needed pretty bad, I didn't question their word.

There was a regular little army of us—fifty or so, best I remember—moving out from Casper toward the town of Buffalo. It was supposed to be a secret, and everybody we come upon was made prisoners to be sure they didn't leak to anybody.

First night's camp, I would of pulled my freight if I hadn't been so broke, and so far from home. The leaders of the army was all drinking and arguing with one another over what to do next. Some of them wanted to go to Buffalo like the plan called for. Some others wanted to go off on a tangent and hit a bunch of rustlers at the cabin of a man by the name of Nate Champion. They figured him for one of the biggest rustlers. They taken a vote, finally, amongst theirselves. We didn't get a vote; we was just the hired hands. A man's reputation back home didn't count for nothing up there. The vote was that we go to Champion's cabin. We had to pack up and leave in the middle of the night.

I was getting to the point in my life where I needed my rest. I sure hadn't had much of it on this trip, and it looked like I wasn't going to get any for a while. I got to thinking to myself that five dollars a day wasn't much. Many's the night I've bet fifty times that much on one hand of cards. If I hadn't been so far from Texas I'd of told them what they could do with all of Wyo-

ming, and I'd of gone south to a warmer climate.

It was a miserable ride, a regular blizzard blowing against us all the way. We stopped to build some fires and thaw out a little then went on to Champion's cabin. We surrounded the layout.

Somebody had made a mistake, not the only one made on that deal by a long shot. There was supposed to be a dozen or more rustlers staying at the place. There wasn't but two, the way it turned out, plus a couple of trappers that had dropped in to get out of the storm. When the trappers came out at daylight, they was made prisoners. They told us there was just two men left inside, Nate Champion and a friend of his called Nick Ray. We had orders to get them dead or alive, best way dead.

Ray came out and looked around, hunting for the trappers, I suppose. Somebody gave an order to fire on him, and a bunch of them did. My hands was so numb from the cold that I couldn't handle my rifle. Ray crawled to the door, and Champion reached out and pulled him in. No telling how many bullets was chipping at the wood all around him, but he didn't let his friend die out there alone.

There wasn't nothing to do but wait. We figured it would be worth a man's life to try to rush that cabin because you would have to cross too much open ground. For five dollars a day they could have it. That feller Champion, somebody said, was an old Texas cowboy. You don't monkey around with that kind until you find out whether they can shoot or not.

By and by somebody came along, one on a horse and one in a wagon. One of the ranchers hollered that the man on the horse was one of those we was supposed to arrest. A lot of shooting broke out, but none of it was any good because both of them got clean away. Everybody's hands was too cold, I reckon; I know mine was.

The wagon had been left behind. We piled it high

with wood, set it afire, and some of the boys run it up against the cabin. Pretty soon the place was burning. We didn't know it then, but Ray was dead. Champion was the only one left alive in there. All of a sudden he busted out running with a rifle in his hands and tried for a ravine. He nearly made it. A couple of the boys was posted back there and brought him down.

I felt kind of low about the whole thing, especially after hearing he was a Texas man. Seemed to me like anybody that game deserved a little more of a show.

But like I say, I was working for wages, and when a man pays me I don't ask a lot of fool questions. I do what he asks me to, or I draw my time.

Seemed to me like we never did stop riding, and the leaders of the crew never stopped bickering and arguing amongst theirselves. That one thing alone was enough to tell me we was in for a hard time. Them two that got away from us was our downfall. They had rode on ahead and given the alarm. We got word that a big gang of rustlers was coming to meet us and would wipe us out like them Indians had done Custer, not too far north of where we was. There was another big argument over whether we ought to go on or back up.

The backer-uppers won. We retreated back to the JA Ranch.

You talk about mad! The cattlemen wasn't half as mad as them rustlers or settlers or whatever they was. They come in on us like a swarm of bees. Before they was through they must of numbered three or four hundred men, which meant there was six or eight of them to every one of us. We forted up at the ranchhouse, and they set up a siege.

We had a good place to make a stand. The house had been built solid, back when people still wasn't sure of the Indians, I reckon, and the logs was thick and square. We found a lot of big timbers and built us up an extra fort outside. We thought we could stand just about anything. But we couldn't. They waited us out,

shooting every time they seen something to shoot at, and lots of times when they didn't. We done the same.

Finally we was about out of ammunition and plumb out of anything to eat. A man can stand up to almost any kind of a fight when his belly's full, but let him get hungry and he falls down on you. Seemed to me about then that the damnfools had taken over, because it was ordered that we would all make a break at the same time and try to shoot our way out of the trap.

I never was one to consider suicide. I've never shot a man I didn't think needed shooting, and I never was that mad at myself. Running out in front of that mob would've been about the same thing as killing yourself, because we'd of lasted about as long as a snowball in a firebox.

Just about the time we was fixing to send ourselves to hell, the army showed up. The cattlemen had friends in high places, but they hadn't come more than five minutes too soon. Any later and they'd of slapped dirt in our faces with a shovel.

Two of the Texas men died of gunshot wounds. I got this bad scar on my cheek from a big splinter, when one of their bullets grazed a log I was behind. We was a pretty hard-used bunch, all in all. They hauled us off to jail. Us Texas boys was moved around from one jail to another and finally even to the state pen while they waited to put us on trial. We hadn't even knowed what the whole thing was about.

The cattlemen that hired us was all out on bail, walking around free and talking big.

The shooting had been in April. We was turned loose on bail finally in August and put on a train for Fort Worth, Texas. We was supposed to go back later for the trial, but I don't suppose any of the boys ever did.

I sure as hell didn't.

Chapter 7

How did I finally come to get into *this* fix? Well, preacher, I'll tell you.

I've had some mighty lean years since that Johnson County episode. I got awful tired of them gun-carrying jobs, but what else could I do? I never did seem to have any more luck with the cards, especially after the years taken to putting arthritis in my joints. Look at them swelled knuckles! Sometimes it's all I can do to even hold a deck, much less to deal with any kind of grace. Old age has its dignity, I reckon, but it's damned inconvenient.

I tried cowboying, but who's going to hire an old man whose joints creak on him when he gets on and off of a horse? And you take most of these cow outfits, they think it's a sin for a hired man to ride anything except a raw bronc. Truth is, they're so tight, most of them, they don't want to buy a horse that costs them over twenty-thirty dollars. Soon as one gets to where he knows something and won't pitch anymore, they

sell him to a farmer. Claim they don't want their cowboys getting lazy. I'm way past the bronc-riding stage,
as you can plainly see.

I tried a little more freelance manhunting, but the
day is over. I even hunted for Butch Cassidy and his
Wild Bunch once, till they crossed over into Wyoming.
I knowed my name was still on the list there, so I
tipped my hat and turned back, hungry.

I done some wolfing for a spell, too. Now *there's* a
dirty job for you, wolfing. But when you look at it,
killing wolves for a bounty ain't much different from
doing it to men, except wolves don't shoot back at you.
Cattlemen had trouble with them big lobo wolves pulling down their calves. And *sheepmen* . . . there just
wasn't no way a sheepman could operate in the same
part of the country with them wolves. They would get
all the lambs first and then take in after the mamas.

A lot of people looked down on the wolfer as a sort
of scavenger, like the men that gathered buffalo bones.
But it was a living. Hard times, a man can't be choicy.

I done a little bartending, one time and another. It's
no life for a man who's known better things. You have
to deal with such a low class of people. Nothing I hate
worse than wrestling with a drunk. The only time I
could ever tolerate a bunch of drunks was when I was
drunk myself. In late years I ain't been that way much.
My stomach's gone to the bad, and it gets real put out
with me when I eat anything or drink anything that it
don't approve of.

So, when you come down to it, there ain't been
much else for me except *pistolero* jobs of one kind or
another. Sometimes I'd get on as a guard for a mine
or a bank or an express company, or for some big-shot
who thought somebody might want to shoot him. Jobs
like that don't have much dignity to them, and you
have to swallow a right smart of dirt.

An old man gets used to a certain amount of dirt,
but not *that* much. I've walked off of jobs and told

them where they could go with it, when I didn't even know where supper was going to come from.

But that gets expensive. Now and again I got so hungry I just had to take a job that I wouldn't otherwise of touched. Like once I was guard to a fat politician from back East who was taking him a long vacation in a big *hacienda* down the river from El Paso. The voters back home was paying his expenses and was being told he was on a long trip out West examining the prison systems. What he was really doing was bathing himself in whiskey and having the women brought to him two at a time, white and Mexican both. It was my job to keep any outsiders from finding him. But one sneaked in anyhow, one of them nosy newspaper reporters. He taken a picture of old Big-Gut with one of the pretty *señoritas* on his lap, and neither one of them wearing anything much except a surprised expression. It run in one of the El Paso papers, and then got back to that politician's home state.

I lost my job, of course. That's another reason I never was partial to them newspaper reporters, always poking around where they ain't got no business.

Them kind of jobs would gag a gut-wagon dog. But when you're in my shape you got to take them or go hungry.

That's why when I got word awhile back that Burney Northcutt wanted to see me at his ranch, I came down here as quick as my little Mexican pony could travel. I remembered how I used to play poker with him in El Paso, back when Lady Luck still approved of me. I remembered how he would cuss and stomp and swear to have me killed, but next time he came to town he'd try to best me again. We wasn't ever what you'd call friendly. In fact, I never did particularly like him. I reckon he felt the same about me. But we had a respect of sorts, one for the other. We was both pretty good at what we done.

I remembered he was a big operator. He came out

into this West Texas country right behind the Indians. He fought old Mother Nature when she was at her meanest, and taken from her when she was at her best. He had carved himself an almighty big country. It wasn't the finest grazing land in Texas; fact is, it's probably some of the sorriest. But it'll do the job if you have enough of it to give your cows plenty of room.

I had heard stories about how he had throwed people off of country he wanted, how he had bought up the law in some counties to where nobody jumped till they heard him holler "frog." But I never gave it much thought because it didn't pertain to me.

But you know, preacher, about Texas and its four-section law? A big part of this land out here belonged to the state, and they passed a law that said a man could homestead four sections of it, and if he could stay there three years without starving to death he could buy it dirt cheap. Well sir, the biggest part of the land that old man Northcutt had, he got on a cheap lease off of the state. When the new law came in, he found people claiming four sections here and four sections there, generally out of the best parts of his ranch. They was four-sectioning him to death. Now, he'd of been right pleased to have bought the whole thing from the state if they'd of let him, but they said he couldn't buy no more than anybody else, which was four sections. Hell, the old man probably had *that* much in corrals.

I got down to the ranch and went to see him. It had been a good many years since we'd laid eyes on each other, and I expect we was both a little surprised. He looked at me real sour-like and says, "By God, Joe Pepper, you've turned into an old man. If I'd of knowed how old you was, I wouldn't of sent for you."

I told him he wasn't apt to turn no schoolgirl's head either.

For a little while I thought I had wasted a long trip. He scowled at me like he was thinking about throwing me off of the ranch. I bristled up a little, just thinking about it. I doubted he had anybody young enough or tough enough to do that to me; I could tell by looking at him that *he* couldn't.

We glared at each other till it seemed like both of our faces would break and fall off. Finally he says, "Well, you ain't likely to scare them with your looks anymore, but maybe you can scare them with your name."

"Who am I supposed to scare?" I asks him.

I didn't know how much raw hate that old man really had in him until he told me about the four-sectioners. I'm glad you wasn't there to hear him, preacher; that language would of shamed you. And the look in his eyes . . . well, I'm not one to scare, but that look made a cold chill run down between these hunched old shoulders. I do believe if he'd of had one of them there in front of us, he would of choked him to death with his hands, or tried to.

I says, "You're hiring me to scare the four-sectioners?"

He cut his eyes at me, and they stabbed like the point of a Bowie knife. "I want you to *kill* one. That'll scare the others."

It had been a good many years since I had killed anybody, though I'd scared a few within an inch of killing themselves. I wasn't sure I needed his money quite that bad. I decided to test him out and see just how serious he was. I says, "You know I'll protect myself if one of them comes at me."

He says, "I want you to make sure one of them *does* come at you. I want you to crowd him till he loses his head, and then you kill him."

I can't say the idea was a new one. But I'd always used it against somebody I figured the world wasn't going to miss, somebody who had it coming to him. I'd never used it against somebody who had done nothing but steal land away from an old thief. Of course I had seldom ever been quite as hungry before as I was right then.

I says, "We ain't talked price yet."

He says, "I ain't got time to horsetrade or quibble with you. It's worth a lot to me to get rid of them nesters, and get rid of them fast." He walked over to his safe. I noticed he didn't move any too quick, and he was dragging his right leg just a touch. The years hadn't been kind to him. If this trouble had come on him twenty years earlier he wouldn't of hired anybody like me to take care of it; he'd of done it for himself.

I could hear his knee joint crack as he eased himself down to work the dial. He gave me a hard look back over his shoulder like he was afraid I'd watch and see the combination. The idea *had* occurred to me, just in case he was a little reluctant afterwards to pay me what he agreed to. I looked off out the window till I heard the door squeal on its hinges. He got out a little tin box and thumped it down on the table. He opened it and taken out a bundle of the prettiest green bills you ever seen. He pitched them across the table at me. "Five hundred dollars now," he says, "and five hundred more when the job is done."

I hadn't seen that much money in one pile in years. My poor old hands began to tremble, just wanting to get in there and feel of the bills, the way when I was younger my hands used to tremble every time they got close to silk. But pardon me, preacher, you wouldn't know about them things.

I wanted to be sure we understood each other. I says, "How will we know when the job is done?"

"When they've buried the nester you shot," he tells me, "and when the rest of them have loaded their wagons and left the country."

I told him I hadn't seen his four-sectioners, but it might be that killing one man wouldn't put them all to flight. I might have to kill more than one. I figured that ought to call for more money.

He cussed a little and told me I was a black-hearted holdup man. I told him that was my natural upbringing, and if I hadn't been that way he wouldn't of wanted to hire me. So he upped the ante. That thousand was to cover the job if it went as easy as he expected it to. He'd put up another five hundred apiece for any extra four-sectioners I had to kill.

Five hundred dollars was probably more than some of them ever got in one bundle in all their lives. Here they was, bringing that much dead.

"All right, done," I tells him. "You got any special man picked out, or do you just want me to shoot one at random?"

That hate came back to him the way I've seldom seen it in a man. He let the breath out between his teeth real slow, and then he says, "There's one. His name is Clayton Massey. You kill *him* and I'll give you a two-fifty bonus."

I drawed old man Northcutt out about this Massey that he seemed to have such a special hate for. Seemed like this was a young fellow from back over in the Concho country. Not only did he have the nerve to come out and file a claim on some of the old man's best water, but he had the extra nerve to bring *sheep* with him. Now, you got to understand that Burney Northcutt was one of them old-time cattlemen who thought all a sheep had to do to ruin a country for fifty years was to walk across it. Sheep outfits trailing west had learned to go forty miles around his place if they wanted to get where they was going without leaving a hundred dead sheep for every mile. The old man had taken a bunch of his cowboys over to throw Massey off of his place, and Massey met them with a gun and a set of state papers out of Austin that said the four sections was his, and he could run anything he wanted to on them . . . even giraffes, if he had any. The old man tried to ride over Massey, and Massey shot the horse out from under him.

The old man owned the sheriff of the county. He had Massey arrested for killing the horse and for trespassing. But the case got transferred out of the county, and the court held that Massey acted in self-defense, and that the old man was lucky it hadn't been him that got shot instead of the horse.

I knowed then why he hated the four-sectioners so bad, especially Massey. What made it even worse was that some of Massey's friends and kinfolks came too, out of the Concho country, and some of them brought sheep as well as cattle. First thing the old man knowed he had him half a dozen little sheepmen sitting on land he thought was going to be his for five hundred years. And it wasn't the nature of them people to homestead the worst land; they always picked the good places, where the water was.

He gives me a description of this young Massey, and how to get to his place, and he tells me, "The quicker you go on over there and kill him, the quicker you can get your extra money and be gone."

I asked him if it would be all right with him if I waited till in the morning. It had been a long ride, and my horse was tired. I was a little weary myself. One thing I didn't want to do was to come up against somebody when I was tired, especially if he had the advantage of being young.

Caution is what makes *old* gunfighters.

I had me a good supper at Burney's expense, a good night's sleep in his bunkhouse, and a good breakfast the next morning. When you get to my age you'll realize how important such small compensations can be. Next morning I set out to Massey's place.

Now, you know this ain't the best ranching country in the world, but I couldn't help thinking as I rode that if my life had taken a different turn in the beginning, I might have had a big spread like Burney Northcutt to pleasure me in my declining years. I wouldn't be riding around all over the country selling my gun to people I didn't particularly like. I'd look at Northcutt's cattle—all colors of the rainbow, half leg and half horn—and think how all this could of been mine. I could understand how he would hate to see it cut up and given to people he didn't think was good enough to shine his boots.

I got to thinking back through all them bygone years. I got to thinking of the time just after the war, and me and Arlee Thompson and our first start, mavericking cattle, making them our own. I thought of me and Millie and our place, of things that hadn't crossed my mind in years and years. A feeling came over me that I'd forgot I ever had, a feeling of being young and having somebody and someplace that belonged to me, something I was a part of, something where I wasn't just an outsider looking in. For a while there it was like I was back in South Texas, and all this was mine, and I wasn't just a lone and lonely old man.

It was a big country, so big that it taken me all morning at a pretty good trot to get to Massey's place. I came to a creek that was the way Northcutt had described it and knowed I was either on the place or close to it. I followed it upstream to the spring where Massey had built him a house. I kept watching all the way for sign of the four-sectioner and his sheep, but I didn't see them. First thing I came to, outside of a scattering of improved Durham cattle, was the house and pens.

You couldn't call it much of a house; there wasn't two wagonloads of lumber in the whole thing. It was one of them little box-and-strip outfits that says "hard times" the minute you look at it. It wasn't more than maybe fifteen feet square, sitting up on sawed-off cedar posts to keep it off of the ground. An old dog came out from under the porch and barked at me. I seen a woman come to the door and stand there, shading her eyes with her hand.

I almost fell out of the saddle.

I tell you, preacher, you couldn't of hit me harder with a tow-sack full of red bricks.

That woman was my Millie, that I had buried nigh forty years ago.

Now, I know you're going to laugh at that, and say it was just an old man's bad eyesight failing on him, and maybe a little of the heat, too. You're going to remind me that I thought the same thing the first time ever I seen Samantha Ridgway. But say what you want to, it happened. There she was, the spitting image.

I rode on up to the house. She spoke to me, but I couldn't hear what she said, and I couldn't say anything back. My tongue was all stuck to the roof of my mouth. She spoke to me two or three times, and finally it got through my thick head that she was telling me to get down and have myself a drink of cool water, because it looked like I was suffering from the heat.

I finally managed to say, "You're Millie!"

She looked kind of surprised. She says, "No, I'm Jill. Jill Massey. I'm afraid you've found the wrong house."

I was still confused. I says, "But you're Millie. Don't you know me?" The whole thing had hit me so sudden that I had a hard time remembering Millie would've been near sixty years old by now, if she had lived. This woman wasn't much over twenty.

I think I must of scared her a little, and that kind of brought me up. I finally got it through my head what she was saying, and that this couldn't be Millie.

I *did* notice then that my head was swimming a little, and that the sweat was running down my face like I'd been caught in a rain. Maybe the heat *had* got me. I eased down from the saddle and leaned against my horse for a minute. I asked her where I could water him, but she told me to go sit in the shade on the step and rest a little. *She* would water him for me.

But first she brought me a dipper of good cool water out of a barrel. I sat down there like she said, and I watched her lead the pony down to the creek and loosen the girth and let him drink. She made him take it slow, which showed she knowed something about horses. Sometimes when they're dry and hot they'll drink enough water to give themselves a bellyache. Same way a man does. I watched her all the time, and I'd swear—if my mind hadn't cleared some—that she was my Millie, born again.

Directly she led the pony up to a corral and pulled the saddle off of him. She turned him loose where he could roll in the dust. She hung the bridle on a post and came back to the house. She says, "You're staying for dinner."

That hadn't been my intention, but I was still too numb to argue. She says, "Clayton'll be in after awhile to eat. He's ranging the sheep over to the east. They won't stray much during the heat of the day."

I'd never made any big study of herding sheep. I didn't care to learn any more about them than I already knowed, which wasn't much. I says. "Where'd you come from, Jill Massey?"

"Over in Concho County," she tells me. "Close to Paint Rock."

I knowed Paint Rock was on the Concho River east of San Angelo, but that didn't answer my question. I says, "I mean, where did you come from originally? Where was you a girl at?"

"Right there," she says. "Where I grew up, you could see the cupola on the Concho County courthouse."

I got to questioning her about her forebears, whether any of them had ever come out of South Texas. I kept thinking maybe she was blood kin of Millie, but as far as I could ever tell, she wasn't. Seems like her folks had come over out of Tennessee before she was born, but after the time of Millie Thompson.

While she was cooking up some red beans and mutton for dinner, I taken my watch out to see what time it was, figuring probably her husband would come riding along pretty soon. All of a sudden I remembered that I carried Millie's picture in the back of the watch. Lord knows how long it had been since I had last looked at it—twenty years, probably. Time does get away from a man. I opened the back. It had been shut so long that I had to prize it with a knifeblade.

There she was, my Millie, just the way I remembered her. Now that I looked at her picture, and compared it to Jill Massey, I could see where this girl didn't look all that much like her after all. Time was playing tricks on me again. When you get old, your mind's eye starts failing on you, same as the ones on the outside.

I got to wondering about myself. I decided I had got to letting my mind wander when I was on the way over from Northcutt's. I had got to thinking about the old days, and I guess without me realizing it, Millie had taken to haunting me again, trying to come to the surface in a way I hadn't let her do in many and many a year. The minute I seen this young woman, I also seen Millie. They wasn't the same atall; they just seemed to be to an old man whose eyes and mind was getting confused.

But I sat and listened to her talk, and it was like it had been the time I found Samantha; the years just rolled away. It was like I was sitting in my own house with Millie again, most of forty years ago. It was like I was a young man, just starting out on the road of life instead of coming up on the end of the trail. For a little while there I think my arthritis quit bothering me, and my shoulders squared up. It was a good feeling.

Her husband came along directly. He seen the strange pony in the corral, and he came rushing to the house to make sure his wife was all right. He seen me sitting there at the table, drinking coffee, and he was sure relieved. I might of been feeling like a young man right then, but all he could see was a harmless coot too old to be a danger to anybody. He shook hands with me and told me he was Clayton Massey, and he hoped I was staying for dinner.

Naturally I was, or my horse wouldn't of been un-
saddled. I didn't tell him my name; I wanted to size
things up first. He would find out soon enough who I
was.

I watched him kiss his wife, kind of gentle and self-
conscious. I had the notion he would of done it some
different if I hadn't been there. That taken me back a
long ways, remembering when it had been the same
with me. I figured him for a man of maybe thirty,
young enough to have all the energy in the world and
old enough to know how to use it.

Jill Massey got dinner finished and put it on the table. She had baked bread in the oven, Mexican style,
flat in the bottom of the pan. Clayton Massey says to
me, "It ain't much, but you're welcome to what there
is. The whole place ain't much yet, but it'll be a lot
more someday when I've had time enough to work on
it."

I got to thinking how he sounded a lot like I had
when I was his age, when I had a pretty woman to
work for, the way he did. By and by I asked him why
he had come way out here instead of staying in Concho
County where he started. He said there wasn't room
anymore. His daddy had settled in that country when
it was still young. Now the son had to move out to a
country that was still young and do like his daddy did.
I pointed out to him that when his daddy went to Concho County there probably wasn't nobody else claiming the land he settled up, except maybe the Indians.
But out here, there wasn't an acre that somebody
hadn't already claimed before him.

He said that was the truth, but the law had decided
it wasn't enough anymore to have all this big open
country in the hands of just a few men. It wanted to
have people settle and towns grow; the frontier was
gone and wasn't coming back. He said the country had
already more than paid the first people here for their
pains, and it was in its legal rights to ask them to move

over and make room. I suppose that made sense to an ambitious young man, but I could also see how it would seem hard to an old mossback like Burney Northcutt who had dripped sweat and sometimes blood all over this land.

I mentioned Northcutt and how I had heard he wasn't too partial to the things that was going on around here, that he felt like they was taking away what belonged to him.

Massey told me a little history that Northcutt had neglected to mention to me. He told me that in the early days there was Mexican settlers—squatters, of course— all up and down these creeks, and Northcutt had come along and run them off. He had even killed a couple or three in the process to show his intentions was serious. He told them their day was over, and it was time for a new deal all around.

Massey says to me, "Now it's *his* day that's over, and it's *us* that have the new deal. You watch, we'll make this country support fifty people for every one that it used to have. This country is meant to grow, not to stand still."

Somehow time kept running backwards for me. I kept thinking about the old times in South Texas, and of the trouble I had with Jesse Ordway over the piece of land that I had and he wanted. I got to trying to see Jesse Ordway in my mind, but it had been so long that I couldn't hardly remember anymore what he looked like. I kept putting Burney Northcutt into the picture in his place.

Massey says, "He's tried a lot of things to get us out of here. He's tried to buy me out, and run me out. He's tried to stampede my sheep, but sheep don't stampede very good. He's tried shooting into them, but he's found I shoot back. He's even had his cowboys ride in here at night and shoot into the house."

I taken a sudden chill. It all came back to me in a rush. I remembered the night they had killed my Millie.

It was forty years ago, but it seemed like it had been yesterday. I closed my eyes and I could hear them riding around the house, shooting into it. In my mind I heard Millie scream. I got to shaking and couldn't quit.

Clayton Massey grabbed hold of me. He says, real worried, "What's the matter, old-timer? Jill, get that bottle of whiskey, quick!"

He handed me the bottle, and I tipped it up and taken a couple of long, hard slugs of it. Gradually I got to feeling warm again, and I quit shaking. He says, "Better take another, old-timer." I told him I had had enough. I tried to get to my feet, but my old knees just couldn't do it. I sat back down and tried to take a grip on myself. I tried to get the old times and the new times separated from one another, so I could think. It was hard, because they was all so mixed up.

Directly I had a grip on myself. The two of them was sitting across the table, looking like I had scared them half to death. With an old man, you never know when he's going to kick over and leave you.

I says, "I'm all right now."

"It's the heat," he tells me. "Man your age has got to watch himself and not overdo it. You better stay with us a day or two and rest. Then you can go on about your business."

I figured it was time to tell him. "I came *here* on business. I came here to kill you."

His mouth dropped open, and his eyes got like a saucer. He shook his head like he didn't believe none of it. "You better go lay down, old-timer. You're sick."

I says, "You ever hear of Joe Pepper, son?"

He nodded his head. "Sure, everybody has. He used to be a gunfighter, long years ago."

"He's *still* a gunfighter," I says. "I'm Joe Pepper."

You know how it is, I reckon, when you have a raving old man on your hands; you try to humor him. The Masseys didn't believe a word of it. I could tell they figured the heat had got me.

Massey says, "Joe Pepper died years ago. He *must* have."

"Not unless I'm a ghost," I tell him.

Gradually he began to come around. I guess there is still a little of the old-time Joe Pepper in my face, if you look hard enough. Finally he gets kind of nervous and says, "Jill, I believe him."

I could tell she did too. All of a sudden I seen fear laying way back deep behind her eyes. Massey taken a quick look toward the corner, where his rifle was propped. He wasn't wearing any pistol; I had taken note of that when he first came into the house. I says, "I wouldn't do what you're thinking, boy. I'd just sit real still."

He didn't look like one who would try to run away. Grab for the rifle, maybe, but not run away. Either choice wouldn't of done him any good if I'd decided to shoot him. He says, "You figuring on killing me right here?"

I says, "That's what I was sent here to do."

"What about Jill?" he says. "Whatever you do to me, don't hurt her, please."

The thought had never entered my mind, but it laid heavy on his. He says, "She's carrying, mister. For God's sake, don't hurt her."

Millie had been carrying, too. I remembered now. Lord, I hadn't even thought of it in years.

The tears commenced to well up in Jill Massey's eyes. She started to plead with me to let her husband be. She said they would move; they would turn this country back to Burney Northcutt if he wanted it so bad.

But Clayton Massey stood up and pushed his chair back. He says to her, "Hush, Jill. Don't you tell him that. The only way Northcutt gets this place is to kill me. I'll never give it to him." He taken a couple of steps backward, and I knowed he was about to make a try for that rifle.

I had real quietly pulled my pistol out of my belt. I brought it up where he could see it real good, and I pushed to my feet. I was afraid my old knees would betray me, but they stood me in good stead. When the pressure comes, I ain't as old as I look. I told Clayton Massey to stand where he was and not do anything that him and me would both be sorry about. I stepped around him, went over to the corner and picked up his rifle. I taken it and pitched it out the door as far as I could.

"Just removing temptation," I tells him. "Thing like that can get a man killed."

By this time I reckon he was convinced that he was as good as dead. He looked at his wife, and back at me, and he says, "If you've got to do it, at least don't do it here in front of *her*. Let's go outside where she doesn't have to see it."

I wasn't going to do it, not there or anywheres else.

I says as harsh as I can, "Now you sit back down at the table and listen to me, boy." He was a little slow about it, so I nudged him with the muzzle of my pistol. "Sit *down*!"

He did. I could see the girl's knuckles as white as flour, gripping her chair. Her face didn't have much more color than that, either.

I says, "Now listen to me, both of you. I said I came here to kill you. But I'm an old man, and an old man's mind is always changing."

"You said Burney Northcutt hired you."

I patted my pocket. "I got the money right here, five hundred dollars."

He says, "You mean you're going to take his money and *not* kill me?"

I shook my head. "No, I'm a professional man. I don't take money on false pretenses. That would ruin my reputation. I'm going to take his money back to him and tell him I've thought it over and changed my mind."

"He won't like it," says Massey. "He's set in his ways."

"He don't *have* to like it. I'll tell him that times have changed for *me*, and they'll just have to change for *him*. I don't like what's happened to me, but I've learned to live with it. He can too."

Jill Massey says, "If he wants my husband dead so bad that he hired you, he'll just go and hire somebody else."

I says, "Not if they know Joe Pepper is here. My name still stands for something in the trade."

Massey says, "What do you mean, if Joe Pepper is here?"

I told him I kind of liked their place, and I was about to be out of a job, and if he could use an old man's help I would hire on real cheap.

He argued that he couldn't pay me much, and I told him an old man didn't need much. A little to eat, a little to drink . . . a lot of time to sit in the sun.

They never did understand what had made me change my mind, and I couldn't tell them because I didn't altogether understand it myself. All I knowed was that them two young people was me and Millie, given another chance to start over. I wasn't going to let Jesse Ordway . . . I mean Burney Northcutt . . . do them out of that chance.

It was a little before dark when I rode up to Northcutt's big frame house. He was sitting on the gallery, taking his evening rest and his pipe. He was some surprised to see me back so quick. He taken his pipe out of his mouth and stared at me. He says, "You always had the reputation of being a fast worker, Joe Pepper. But damn if that ain't the fastest five hundred dollars I ever spent. I reckon you've come for the rest?"

I reached in my pocket and taken out the roll of greenbacks that had felt so good in my hands. I pitched it over into his lap. I says, "No, I come to give your money back to you. I don't take pay if I don't do a job."

I reckon it was typical of him that he thought the worst. "Taken a look at it and got cold feet, did you? I ought to've knowed better than to hire a man that's got so old the nerve has gone out of him. Time the word gets around about this, there won't nobody hire you to slop hogs."

I shrugs my shoulders and tells him, "Don't matter, I already got work."

"Doing what?" he says real nasty. "Washing out spittoons in a bar?"

"Herding sheep," I tells him.

He stood up, and when he did I seen the pistol in his boottop. An old badger like Burney Northcutt wasn't going to get caught without a six-shooter, not even on his own front gallery. He says, "You sold out. I've heard of you doing lots of things, Joe Pepper, but I never heard of you double-crossing anybody before."

I says, "I never needed to before, Jesse."

It occurred to me that I had called him by the wrong name, but somehow it didn't matter. Standing there like he was, he looked to me like Jesse Ordway of almost forty years ago. All of a sudden the front gallery of that old ranchhouse was the bank where I had met Jesse. I was a young man again, and full of grief and anger because I had just buried a young wife that I had loved, and Jesse Ordway was the man who had been the cause of it.

Burney Northcutt reached down for the pistol, but it wasn't Burney Northcutt I shot . . . it was Jesse Ordway. I shot him once and seen him fall back against the wall, and all the grief and the anger and the pain came rushing up from forty years' burying, and I shot him again, and again and again. I kept shooting till the pistol was empty.

I could hear men hollering around me. I was still in that South Texas town, running for my horse. I got on him and started down the street, only it wasn't really a street atall, it was just a ranch yard. I managed to get some cartridges back into the gun and shoot at Jesse Ordway's men who was shooting at *me*. I looked around for Felipe Rios, but he wasn't there. I couldn't understand why he wasn't; he was *supposed* to be.

They came after me, but I was still ahead of them when dark came.

I wasn't familiar with the country. I rode way into the night, trying to tell myself I wasn't lost but knowing I was. Finally these weary bones had all they could stand, and I had to get down and stretch out on the ground and rest.

I remember dreaming a lot through the night. There was a woman . . . she was Millie awhile, and then she was Samantha, and then she was Jill Massey, but always the same woman. And there was me and Clayton Massey, all mixed up with one another so that I never did know for sure which one of us was which.

Finally I felt something touch me. I opened my eyes to the sunlight, and there was a man leaning over me. He had just lifted the pistol out of my belt. He had a badge on his shirt. It looked as big as a washtub. So did the muzzle of the rifle he held down to my nose. I seen then that he had a bunch of men with him, all of them pointing guns at me.

Well sir, that's how come me to be where I am now. They hauled me here and throwed me in this jail. Ordinarily there wouldn't of been a term of court for two months, but because old man Northcutt was a power in this country, and because Joe Pepper had a name for himself too, they rushed things a mite. They brought in a district judge that Northcutt had helped get elected, and picked them a jury of Northcutt cowboys.

It didn't make no difference to them that the Northcutt power died when he did. Without him, the old ranch of his won't be long in breaking up. The people who talk so bitter about me killing him won't let him get cold in the grave till they start filing on his lands to grab what they can of the leavings.

Clayton Massey came in and testified about North-cutt hiring me to kill him, and me changing my mind. That didn't change the jury's mind, though. They'll all be out of work pretty soon on account of me. They'll have to be drifting off and hunting jobs somewhere else, unless they decide to file on four sections of Northcutt land themselves.

That's about all there is to the story, preacher. I don't know if I've told you what you wanted to find out.

They've finally quit hammering on that scaffold out on the square. I reckon they got it finished.

I feel kind of sorry for them boys, having to work on it most of the night. They'll be disappointed when they come down here in the morning and find out they won't get to use it after all.

That noise out yonder? Just some friends of mine, come to get me a change of venue. Friends of yours, too, I expect, so if you recognize any of them I'd be obliged if you keep quiet about it. I wouldn't want to get them four-section people in trouble.

Better stand back here against the door, preacher, away from the outside wall. They're fixing to pull the window bars out with that team of mules, and I'd hate to have a stone fall on your foot and cripple you.

There it goes. Mind giving me a lift up through that hole?

Well, been nice talking with you, preacher, but I got to be hurrying along. Tell the boys I'm real sorry about their jail. Next time they ought to build it stronger. This one won't even hold an *old* man!